D1015607

DEATH ON TUCKERNUCK

DEATH ON TUCKERNUCK

FRANCINE MATHEWS

**SOHO
CRIME**

Published by
Soho Press, Inc.
227 W 17th Street
New York, NY 10011

Library of Congress Cataloging-in-Publication Data

Mathews, Francine, author.
Death on Tuckernuck / Francine Mathews.
Series: The Merry Folger Nantucket mysteries; 6

ISBN 978-1-61695-993-7
eISBN 978-1-61695-994-4

1. Murder—Investigation—Fiction. 2. Women detectives—Fiction.
3. Mystery fiction.
LCC PS3563.A8357 D46 2020 | DDC 813/.54—dc23

Printed in the United States of America

10 9 8 7 6 5 4 3 2 1

This book is offered to the men and women of the Nantucket Police, the EMTs and firefighters, the Harbormaster and Coast Guard, the Selectmen and -women, the gardeners and landscape pros, builders and tradesmen, sanitation workers and restaurant chefs, waitstaff and bartenders, the writers and booksellers, reporters and broadcasters, doctors and nurses and therapists and social workers, the pilots and marine captains, taxi drivers and shopkeepers, farmers and clergy, fishermen and artists and musicians and jewelers and basket-makers, the philanthropists and organizers, and all of the coaches and teachers—Nantucket's caretakers, all.

Without responsibility, there would be no care. Without care, there would be no community—just a storm-lashed island in the midst of an endless sea.

DEATH ON TUCKERNUCK

Prologue

HE HADN'T EXPECTED Ash that Saturday morning, hurrying down the weathered wooden pier in her rope-soled wedges and skinny jeans, a slouchy silk sweater slipping down to reveal one perfect shoulder. He hadn't expected the way his stomach seized and his throat constricted at the sight of her blunt-cut brown hair, swinging glossily just below her chin, or the stab of pain when her eyes slid past him and widened happily at the sight of Matt on the main deck. It was Matt she waved to, not him; Matt who took control, leaping to the stern to extend a hand for Ashley's canvas tote and her rolling overnight bag.

"Welcome aboard," Matt said, teeth flashing in his tanned face. It might have been a beer commercial, the gorgeous girl stepping onto the three-million-dollar yacht and into the arms of the hunk with money to burn. In a second, the guitars would crash and the camera would switch to the pair of them high in a hot-air balloon, fingers hooked around longnecks. Or a rave on a tropic beach under the stars, both of them barefoot in the sand.

—While he stood paralyzed, the third wheel, his mind racing in search of a way out. Staring dumbly at Ash, the unforeseen complication. Which is what she'd always been.

"I thought you had to work today," he attempted. "I thought you were on the weekend schedule."

"Jen offered to cover," she said simply, and turned to grin at Matt. "What fool would pass up an invitation like this?"

"This" being *Shytown*, a Hatteras M75 Panacera, complete with an elegant main cabin seating area, state-of-the-art galley, and a lower deck fitted with staterooms for eight. Which he and Matt intended to power up the coast from its Long Island slip to Martha's Vineyard and then Provincetown over the next week, stopping at Block Island along the way.

He watched Ashley drop her canvas bag on the stern lounge and hug Matt. Matt's hands skimmed her hips. A halo of midafternoon sun seemed to bind them, the kind of light that always blurred his vision when Ash appeared.

Could this get any worse?

"Somebody needs a drink." Matt was smiling into Ash's eyes as though she hadn't screwed up their plans entirely. Had he invited her *knowing* she was scheduled to work, and assumed she'd say no? Or had he been drunk when he asked?

"Follow me." Matt grabbed Ash's suitcase and ducked down the gangway that led to the lower deck. "We'll stow your stuff in the aft stateroom. It's the largest."

Matt's stateroom, of course. Would he be moving to a guest cabin? Unclear. He'd probably wait and see how the day went. How easily the steaks and lobster tails sizzling on the Weber grill, the endless vault of stars overhead and the reggae on *Shytown's* expensive sound system, persuaded Ashley to share her mattress.

Cursing under his breath, he moved forward to the bow and began to loosen the mooring hitch, glancing as he did so at the horizon. Clear as glass. The swells were gentle. A slight breeze caressed his cheek. Unbelievably gorgeous weather, in fact, for late September. Matt always expected him to plot their course well in advance for these runs, building in options for alternative stops and routes, which meant studying not only charts and GPS but checking the NOAA weather forecasts, and calculating what all of it might mean for *Shytown's* schedule over the next several days.

Because Matt trusted him like blood.

He'd earned that trust over the past year. And he'd done his homework for the coming week. Then he'd carefully arranged his lies.

"Hey, man!" Matt yelled from the flybridge. "We good?"

"Aye, aye," he called back, coiling the mooring line on the deck cleat. The twin diesel engines purred to life. In a matter of seconds, *Shytown* slid cleanly out of the marina slip and headed for the channel.

Ashley joined him, a salt-rimmed margarita glass in her hand. "Want one? There's a whole pitcher."

"Not when I'm crewing, Ash."

She pecked him on the cheek. "You're so responsible. This boat is *fabulous*. Like something out of a movie."

"Indeed it is," he agreed.

And promised himself he'd keep her alive.

Chapter One

DIONIS MATHER PULLED the hood of her oil-stained gray sweatshirt over her tousled black ponytail. The wind was rising off Madaket Harbor and the temperature falling as five o'clock closed in. Gooseflesh rose on her bare calves. She huddled on the seat of her beat-up fiberglass work skiff and vigorously rubbed the chilled skin her cutoffs had left exposed.

It had been sunny and hot during the multiple runs she'd made that day to Tuckernuck, the small island trailing like an afterthought off the western end of Nantucket Island. She'd rejoiced in the wind and salt spray that ripped past the gunwales of the boat, because it felt like summer on the water—without the dense traffic of Summer People. There was all the bliss of the deep emerald sea arrowing from the bow and the curve of Nantucket's western shoreline, the throttle under her palm and the narrow black band of Tuckernuck coming up on the horizon. Not another craft in sight. Until the clouds rolled in, Dionis had been happy.

She and her dad, Jack Mather, ran a family business that kept them plying the waters between the two islands for at least six months each year. Tuckernuck was a private place off the electrical and cyber grid. There were no paved roads, no market, no bar or restaurant, not even a beachside kiosk selling coffee. No clam shack, no gas station, no place to buy suntan lotion or a boxed lunch or rent a beach chair—and only a handful of ancient cars with their noses tipped into the dunes. Cell phone coverage was sporadic, and internet nonexistent. What Tuckernuck *did* offer was roughly 900 acres of gloriously pristine beaches, ocean views, and moorland, privately owned by the families who'd built its houses. Some of those houses were brand new, and some of them were centuries old. None of the folks who'd inherited Tuck's isolation and privilege lived on the island past mid-October, and only a few owned boats for independence.

The rest relied on Dionis and Jack Mather—Tuckernuck caretakers—for almost everything they needed to survive: deliveries of milk, fresh produce, and bread. Packages from the Nantucket post office; toilet paper and kerosene for storm lamps; lawn mowers, for those indulgent enough to lay sod in front of their ancient saltboxes; sod brought over on the Mathers' construction barge. Batteries; cases of wine, vodka, and beer; bottled water. Steak. Salad dressing. Playing cards. Roof shingles, and panes of glass for replacing broken windows. I-beams and insulation for new additions. Dog food and trash bags. Solar panels, for those who disdain propane generators. Propane, for those who mistrust solar. Down comforters. Citronella candles and insect repellant. Outdoor table umbrellas and rose secateurs. Guests and their baggage—both physical and spiritual—delivered by golf cart from the Tuckernuck Lagoon's dock. Sometimes the Mathers even ferried medical technicians from Nantucket, to evacuate the sick to Cottage Hospital.

Today, on a Sunday at the tail end of September, only a few of Tuckernuck's houses were still inhabited. Dionis and Jack had been doing mostly end-of-season maintenance runs. Pulling garbage. Tidying flower beds. Draining the plumbing systems of the houses already vacated for the winter, so that pipes did not freeze and burst. Easy work, in Dionis's estimation, after the craziness of July and August.

But now she was cold and the transient happiness of sun on water had fled from her veins. Her muscles were sore. She wanted a beer. And her father was late picking her up at Jackson Point.

The sound of a truck engine drew her head around. Dionis rose to her feet, following the battered Dodge Ram with narrowed eyes as it lurched past the entrance to the Jackson Point lot and came further on, swaying to a halt at the boat landing's edge.

Her father jumped out, leaving the driver's side door open. "Hey," he said. "Let me give you a hand."

She was already lifting some of the knotted plastic bags of garbage from the belly of the work skiff, swinging them toward Jack, who grunted as he hoisted them into his truck's flatbed. A week's worth of trash—some of it the unholy detritus that surfaced at the end of the season—had to be delivered to Nantucket's public waste and recycling center. The bags were already sorted and separated by garbage type: compost, landfill, plastic, and glass. This was the third load Dionis had brought across Madaket Harbor today.

"Temperature's dropped," she observed.

Jack scanned the sea, noting the freshening chop. Crow's feet tightened at the corners of his faded blue eyes. "Nor'easter in the forecast."

"You're kidding." Dionis frowned. "It's way too early in the season, Dad."

"Climate change." Her father shrugged. "Sea's getting warmer, weather's getting weirder. Seasons don't mean anything now, you know that."

She hoisted the last bag of trash and glanced over her shoulder, toward the town of Nantucket some six miles to the east. Its gray-shingled landscape was impossible to pick out beyond the clutter of new buildings on the Madaket shoreline. But the sky was still relatively clear in that direction.

"I'll believe it when I see it," she said skeptically.

"You do that." Jack grinned at her. "Nothing's like it used to be. Remember the polar vortex?"

Involuntarily, Dionis shivered. The previous winter had been brutal. Madaket Harbor froze solid between Jackson Point and Tuckernuck, the ice wave reaching so far inland on the Nantucket shore it had swamped the thresholds of houses. It was true; everything seemed more volatile these days, more extreme. But nor'easters usually didn't hit until well into fall.

"They say there's a chance this one misses us," her father added as she joined him in the cab of the truck.

"LET'S PUT THE table between the sofa and the windows," Meredith Folger suggested, her hands on her hips. One long strand of blonde hair had escaped from its clip and was grazing her chin in a way Peter Mason was tempted to fix, but her green gaze was focused on the bare floor and her lips were set in a firm line. She screamed efficiency and purpose. He knew better than to trifle with either.

Peter surveyed the half-empty living room of the two-hundred-year-old captain's house. He and Merry were readying themselves for an onslaught of wedding guests. There were nearly a hundred expected in the house Saturday for the reception after the ceremony in the Congregational church, but Peter's family arrived Thursday and would expect food and beds in the ancestral Mason home. Merry wanted it to feel welcoming. She had already banished a pair of heavy Victorian upholstered rockers and a matching love seat—all of them hideous and uncomfortable, but tolerated by habit—to the attic. As neither Peter nor Merry actually *lived* in the white clapboard mansion on Cliff Road, and both worked full time, he as a farmer and she as a police detective, they had crammed their weekend with far too much lifting.

"You mean, the *dining* room table?" Peter had hidden under the mahogany Chippendale as a boy, the sunburned legs of various adults a sprawling stockade that protected him from the world. The difference between the table's scarred and cracked underside and its glowing surface was an early lesson: things were more complicated than they looked, and rewarded inspection.

"The oak trestle table from the hallway," Merry corrected patiently. "It'll work for family dinners in here, in front of the fire."

"We're using the dining room on Saturday, though, right?"

"Just for cocktails. A small-plates buffet. Tess is serving the sit-down dinner outside. The tent people start setting up their poles tomorrow."

Tess da Silva was one of their dearest friends, a restaurant owner recruited to cater the reception. The tent people were coming because Peter's sister, Georgiana, had convinced Merry to lay down a dance floor and to cover the rear garden with billowing acres of draped canvas. The tent would block half the house's spectacular view of the granite jetties sweeping into Nantucket Sound, but weather was too variable on the island in late September to risk an unprotected party.

"Once your sister gets here Thursday, we need a place where everyone can gather. The kitchen's too small."

She was right, of course—Georgiana was bringing her husband and four kids. The kitchen was an old-fashioned galley, long overdue for a complete renovation—*if* any of the Masons ever decided to inhabit the house full-time. For all its history and grandeur, the Cliff Road place was used solely for a few weeks each July and August, the family's real lives being led elsewhere. Only Peter had made Nantucket his permanent home—and he lived miles outside of town at Mason Farms, surrounded by the shifting beauty of the moors and his cranberry bogs, his sheep and the transient cloudscapes that swept over the island.

"This room will feel more casual if we eat in here—more welcoming," Merry persisted. "We can use the side chairs from the kitchen and those matching ones at the ends."

She gestured toward a pair of faded, sea blue wing chairs positioned on either side of the hearth. Peter could not remember ever sitting in them. But he could see a shadow of his dead father now in the one on the left, grasping the arms like a throne.

The two of them lifted books, pewter candlesticks, crystal hurricane lanterns, and a decorative porcelain flower bowl from the oak trestle in the hall, piling them willy-nilly on some Windsor chairs. Then they hoisted the table and carried it carefully into the airy living room.

"Right here," Merry ordered. "Ranged along the front windows. Leave enough space on each side for all of us to squeeze in."

Peter obliged, then stood back and surveyed the effect. The windows were draped in fern-colored silk. Two worn linen sofas, liberally strewn with squishy needlepoint pillows worked by generations of Mason women, flanked the large open fireplace. Woven mohair throws from Nantucket Looms lay folded on their rounded arms. The trestle table sat perpendicular to these, exposed to the warmth of a log fire and anyone casually grouped around it. The previous summer, Georgiana had swapped out the frayed Chinese carpets that some forgotten Mason whaling captain had brought back from a Pacific voyage for a thick rectangle of woven sisal. The heavy mat would absorb salt air, sand, and sound.

Merry unfurled an embroidered linen runner down the length of the table and set the hurricanes and the porcelain bowl in its center. "A few dahlias from the garden, and we're good."

"The room feels less fussy," Peter admitted. "I might actually like being in here."

It was, he supposed, a metaphor for his life. Once he'd met Meredith a few years before, all that was rigid in his mind and soul had gradually relaxed into something far healthier. Almost, but not quite, as effortlessly as moving the table—it began, he thought, with seeing his space differently. As mutable rather than fixed. Open to change, instead of resistant to it.

"Your mother will hate how I've messed with her house," Merry said.

"Yes, she will." He reached out and pulled her into the crook of his shoulder, where her head briefly rested. Julia Mason stood for all that was most constricting and suffocating in Peter's life. She was sarcastic, unrelenting in her criticism, and convinced that by choosing Merry, her son was marrying beneath him. She once used the archaic term mésalliance, and when Peter exploded, shrugged that Merry would never understand the word anyway. His mother's impending arrival to the island was tiresome but necessary; Peter refused to let it ruin his happiness. He had allowed Julia to ruin too many things in the past.

"Will it be a problem?" Merry asked. "If your mom's annoyed?"

"Not for me." He touched her forehead, smoothing away a pucker of concern with one fingertip. Merry was looking tired. She had to work a full shift starting at 6 A.M. the next morning. At this rate, she'd be exhausted by Saturday. She was still the most beautiful thing he'd ever seen.

"Do you know that I can't wait to marry you?" he asked.

Merry kissed him, and moved without another word to gather up the books they'd piled on the hallway chairs.

He was skinning and boning the bluefish he'd caught that afternoon off Watch Hill when Ashley found him at the stern.

"I wish you'd teach me how to do that," she said, as he slid the narrow steel blade between the flesh and the skin. "You make it look easy. Then again, you make everything look that way."

He shrugged. "It's a knack. Not a skill." Ash would never know how hard he worked to look effortless. Or what it cost him.

"How'd you two meet?" she asked, with a slight tilt of her chin toward the flybridge above. Matt stood at the controls, intent on reaching Oak Bluffs tonight, unable to hear them.

"I don't even remember anymore," he said.

"I think you're lying. Why would you lie to me?"

He lifted his eyes from the fillet. She was staring at him, really seeing him, for the first time in weeks.

"You knew him in Chicago. Didn't you?"

Her words were as targeted as bullets. No fool, Ash, though she sometimes tried to look that way.

"Yes," he told her. And tossed the bones overboard.

Chapter Two

"WE'RE GOING TO have to get everybody off," Jack Mather declared flatly that Monday morning. He was sitting on a barstool when Dionis padded into the kitchen, still in her pajamas, dark hair streaming down her back. It was a little after 7:30 A.M. and the thick smells of burnt coffee and crisp maple bacon suggested winter to her nose. The opaque gray light beyond the small window over the kitchen sink deepened the idea. *Fog.* The weather had changed. Autumn was here.

"It's not going away—just getting bigger."

"What is?"

Jack set down his coffee mug and sighed. "The nor'easter I told you about."

"I thought it was supposed to dodge us. Head north."

"It did," he agreed, "where it ran smack into the remnants of a tropical storm off the coast of Labrador and turned into something much nastier. It's a Cat Two right now and circling back toward us."

"A hurricane?" Dionis echoed in disbelief. "They never hit New England."

Her father slid his bulk off the stool and shuffled around to the coffee maker. "Oh, I wouldn't go that far. But the last time something like this happened was in '91. You were pretty young, then."

Four years old, Dionis thought. *When Mom left.*

"I'm not surprised you don't remember."

"You mean the Perfect Storm," she said quietly. The name a journalist and Hollywood had given it. The remnants of a tropical storm and a nor'easter had collided in the North Atlantic. It had been deadliest offshore.

Jack handed her a fresh mug of coffee, black the way she liked it. She and her dad were roughly the same height; her eyes met his over the mug's rim—blue eyes, worn as old denim.

"They're tracking it, right," she said tentatively. "So, we'll know when and where it's going to hit."

"It's headed southeast, but expected to circle back west. Right now, the National Weather Service is predicting landfall at New Bedford or Rhode Island. Some day this week."

"South of us," Dionis pointed out. "We'll just get a ton of rain."

"Maybe. Or maybe it turns west early—and makes landfall here. We have to evacuate Tuckernuck regardless, Di. Packing up the folks still left out there, and shutting down all the houses, will take every hour we've got left."

Dionis thought of the undulating terrain of the smaller island, the way most of the homes were positioned on heights in the moors for the best possible view of the surrounding ocean. Hurricane winds would lift off a few roofs, and smash a lot of windows unless they could get them boarded up in time. Even then, a few of the houses— abandoned family properties, rarely inhabited—were in poor condition, just begging to be trashed by a violent cyclone. The Mathers couldn't do much about those; they weren't responsible for them. But if their clients' houses were damaged, they'd be held accountable. Jack Mather was paid to provide off-islanders with peace of mind.

"I get it," she muttered. "Even if it's a false alarm, we have to act like it's a crisis. We'll take a financial hit if we're not all over this."

"Sooner rather than later. If the seas get too high for the work skiffs to navigate . . ." Jack glanced at his watch. "Be ready to leave in half an hour, okay? We'll go house-to-house, figure out who's still on Tuck and tell everybody we meet that they've got to be packed up and ready to leave by tomorrow afternoon, Wednesday morning at the latest."

"I'll print up a notice we can drop at each door," Dionis suggested, "in case we miss somebody."

"Good idea. While you're doing that, I'll go get gas."

Jack intended to fill his supply of ten-gallon plastic containers with fuel to carry over to Tuckernuck. He kept a second truck parked on the island specifically for house calls, and it didn't run on air.

He paused, already lost in plans, his right hand rubbing his left bicep.

"Pull something yesterday?" Dionis asked.

He shrugged. "I've got all winter to heal."

Dionis swallowed the last of her coffee. Her laptop was in her bedroom. As the screen door slammed behind her father, she ran upstairs and switched it on.

"WHAT ARE YOU doing at your desk?" Howie Seitz demanded. "You're getting married, girl."

Merry looked up from her computer screen at the tall, lanky sergeant, who was lounging in her doorway. She could absolutely have taken off the week before her wedding without disturbing the balance of life in the Nantucket Police Department. The crazed demands of summer, with its dense traffic, bicycle and scooter accidents, lost children, occasional drunk, or college kid high on Ecstasy, were hard to recall this last week of September. Nantucket wasn't quite as dead as it was in, say, January. September was considered one of the most beautiful months for people free of school-age children to visit the island. But it was downright relaxed compared to July. Merry and Peter had planned their wedding for a month after Labor Day for exactly that reason: she had expected to be completely free.

"Nice haircut," she observed, eyeing Seitz. He'd lost about four inches from his unruly mop of black curls and the strong features of his tanned face were newly visible, newly arresting. But there was a certain grimness to the straight line of his mouth that set off a warning bell in Merry's mind. Was Howie unhappy? Feeling unwell? Under financial pressure? With a slight shock, she realized that the kid she thought of as just out of college—they had first met when Howie landed on Nantucket as a sophomore in Northeastern University's Criminal Justice program—was roughly two years shy of thirty. The frustrating sidekick had become her trusted partner. She should find time to sit down with him outside of work and assess how he really was.

Howie glanced over his shoulder and then, satisfied no one could overhear him, leaned further into her room. "The chief informed me that long hair was no credit to the force," he muttered. "This isn't a style choice. It's job security."

Merry sighed. "Yeah, well, he told *me* I could only have two weeks off to get married. It's hard enough to celebrate with friends *and* see three European capitals in that amount of time, so I'm taking shifts straight through Thursday. I'd be working Friday, if there weren't the minor matter of a wedding rehearsal to attend. And my toenails to polish. Why don't you tell Pocock to go to hell and get a job on the mainland, Seitz?"

"Why don't you quit, Mer? You're only marrying ten million bucks!"

"At *least*," Merry agreed. "But I like my job."

"So do I," Howie retorted. "As long as you're here, I'm staying. Call in sick Thursday."

"I might. Think the chief would notice?"

Howie grinned. "I think he'd fire you. Which would solve all our problems."

"Careful what you wish for." Merry winked at him. "I feel a stomach virus coming on."

"I INTEND TO ride out this storm, missy," Honoria Cabott declared, "and Jorie with me, thank you very much."

She was a white-haired wisp of a nonagenarian with a will like iron, standing firmly at the end of her driveway and refusing passage to Jack Mather's truck. Her great-grandparents had made the daring decision in 1881 to leave their house on Union Street and build a new home on Tuckernuck. Society on Nantucket, they thought, had become *too swollen with interlopers* from the Mainland. *New-monied upstarts with no Quaker history*, forcing their way into the island's Establishment. The Cabotts had raised eight children, a henhouse full of chickens, and every conceivable vegetable at their homestead on Tuckernuck. Honoria had actually attended the one-room school house that educated Tuckernuck's children in the Depression years when the small island's residents braved the winters and lived year-round in their homes. Now, she spent October to April in an assisted-living facility on Nantucket; but from May through Columbus Day Weekend, her paid companion, Jorie Engstrom, kept her safe and kept her company in the Cabotts' westward-facing saltbox. It was named Vineyard View. On clear days, Honoria insisted she could see Martha.

"I understand, Miss Cabott." Dionis jumped down from her father's battered truck and tentatively touched the elderly woman's shoulder. It felt like a bird's wing beneath her hand. "It's hard to say goodbye to summer. I feel it myself. But we're talking about a hurricane. No one knows how strong it might be, and you're in danger here with the house unprotected on this bluff."

"The house has seen worse. I remember the Great New England Hurricane of '38." Honoria folded her arms, tanned and wrinkled as aged leather, across her chest. "Nobody cut and ran from that one, and it was fierce! Made the war that came after seem like child's play."

"I'm sure you've weathered a lot of wind and rain over the years," Dionis agreed. "But nobody else will be left on Tuckernuck by Wednesday night, ma'am, and it could be frightening all alone out here with no one to help you."

"I've got canned goods," Honoria countered. "And kerosene."

"Which could burn your house down, if the wind blows out your windows," Dionis returned matter-of-factly.

"Board 'em up, then. That's what I pay your father for!"

"We plan to, ma'am. But the boards will stay up all winter once they go on. You'll be living in darkness for the rest of the time you stay in the house."

Honoria's erect spine sagged slightly and her arms fell to her sides. "Why does the summer always end too soon?"

"It happens faster each year, doesn't it?" Dionis smiled at her.

Jack Mather stuck his head out the truck window. "We'll be back Wednesday morning to move you out, Miss Cabott."

Honoria shook her head. "I never know—once I'm back in that *facility* for the winter—" she said with distaste, "—if I'll ever get out again. And I don't mean in a pine box."

"I understand," Dionis repeated. She didn't, really. She was twenty-nine years old and couldn't imagine living nearly a century. But she glanced at Jorie Engstrom, Honoria's companion, who was standing behind the older woman, a few feet further up the drive. She was half Honoria's age, with a thick plait of Nordic blonde hair sweeping down her back.

Jorie mouthed something at Dionis.

We'll be ready.

"YOU WANTED TO see me, sir?"

Bob Pocock never lifted his eyes from his computer screen. Merry counted to seventeen before he said, "Seen today's weather report?"

"Not yet. Sir."

The chief's lips quirked. "I'd have thought the anxiety of a weekend wedding would have you on constant internet refresh."

She was tempted to tell him that she'd ordered a tent for that very reason—so she didn't have to worry about rain or sun in the few hours of freedom he'd granted her before Saturday—but Merry stayed silent. Goading Pocock was pointless.

"National Weather Service has issued a hurricane warning," he murmured. "Could make landfall south of here by Thursday."

Damn. That was when Peter's family was supposed to arrive. "I see. Landfall where, exactly?"

"Rhode Island. New Bed. Either way, we'll get serious rain and wind. Storm surge, undoubtedly. The streets near the wharves will flood."

The lower end of town was increasingly awash during nor'easters, as the climate changed and weather grew more extreme. On multiple occasions during the previous year, Merry had waded through water up to her knees, as though the island were part of the Venice lagoon. She didn't remember that happening as often when she was a child. Erosion of the island's Atlantic beaches was a constant threat during extreme storm events, too, with the foundations of vulnerable houses undercut by massive surf and entire dunes washed out to sea. But hurricanes were exponentially worse than nor'easters. She tried to recall the last one that had struck the islands—Bob, wasn't it?

"Are they talking categories, yet?"

"It's just a Cat Two at the moment. Could be a Three, however, by the time it reaches us. That means wind speeds between roughly a hundred ten and a hundred thirty miles per hour."

Good lord, she wouldn't even be able to *put up* a tent, with that kind of gale blowing—

"I've put Scott Tredlow on alert"—Scott was the Nantucket Police Department's emergency management coordinator—"and I've placed some calls to my opposite numbers at the Fire Department and Public Works," Pocock added.

"Are you planning to call an Interdepartmental Preparedness Meeting, sir?"

The chief's flat gray eyes drifted up to hers. "I already have, detective. It's in twenty-two minutes. I am, after all, the emergency management director."

His tone was sarcastic, but Merry had learned that Pocock turned snarky only when he felt insecure and defensive. He was a Chicago native who'd come around the Point—as Nantucketers referred to those who moved full-time to the island—barely six months before. Did he know that Nantucket had been the first town on both the Cape and Islands to win a "StormReady" designation from the National Oceanic and Atmospheric Agency because of its high level of emergency preparedness? Was Pocock dialed-in enough to understand which neighborhoods were designated zone A in a major storm event—priority evacuation targets—and others zone B, Merry wondered? On an island, it might seem obvious that the coastline and Nantucket Harbor were vulnerable to massive flooding. But so, too, was everything around Madaket Harbor and Hummock Pond, on the southwest end of the island. And all of Tuckernuck, Merry knew, was zone A—an evacuation priority.

Tuckernuck. Was anybody even still living out there this late in September? And how, short of sending a police launch across the water to check, would they know? Tuck was private property. The police only set foot on it if called to a crime or accident scene. Merry made a mental note to ask Scott Tredlow if he'd contacted any Tuckernuck caretakers. The people paid to safeguard the smaller island would have their fingers on its pulse.

"I realize relief ops aren't your responsibility, detective," Pocock was saying, "but you're a native who's seen a few decades of island weather. I want you at this meeting."

"Of course, sir." She hesitated, then said, "Sergeant Tredlow has briefed you, I assume, on Nantucket's key vulnerabilities?"

"I would guess they're much like any coastal town's." The chief lifted his brows as though waiting for her to wow him.

"Yes, sir. With a few added quirks for good measure. Our power sources are distinctly vulnerable to storm surge—"

"Because the electrical substation is located in a flood zone," Pocock finished sarcastically. "Yes—I think the whole town is aware of that."

"And two fairly old undersea cables connect the substation to its actual source of power," Merry persisted, "which is thirty miles across the sound, on Cape Cod."

"That's why we have backup generators." Pocock hunched closer to his screen, as though shielding himself from her words. "On higher ground."

There were two backup systems—one, an ancient diesel generator, and the other, a state-of-the-art Tesla battery array. "Those function best, sir, as stopgap assistance if one of the cables is disrupted. If both cables are damaged by storm surge . . ."

"We'll be without power for some time," Pocock concluded.

"Which will affect certain services most. Medical care, for one—"

"They deliberately built the new hospital with its own propane backup generators," Pocock objected.

"—and assisted living facilities, for another. But I'm sure you'll be talking about all of this at the interdepartmental meeting, as well as the potential for toxic sewage resurgence from drain flooding throughout the streets of town."

Shit on the cobblestones. There was a brief pause, as Pocock debated possible retorts. All he said was, "Anything else, detective?"

"Boats." Merry kept her eyes trained on the window beyond the chief's head.

"Meaning?"

"There are a lot still moored in the Boat Basin, Children's Beach, all over Polpis and Monomoy . . . and at the Town Pier. Probably out at Madaket, too. I assume the harbormaster will be at your meeting—but we should send a pair of uniforms to each of those dock areas *right now*, to walk the slips and warn anybody living on board their vessels. They'll need to get themselves and their boats out of the water."

"We can use Ping alerts for that," Pocock said. The Town of Nantucket had adopted an app for texting emergency information to islanders' cell phones.

"That should work, for those who've downloaded

the app." Of course, this infuriating man—patronizing, chilly, and in Merry's opinion, misanthropic—would rely on a tech solution to handle human suffering. It would be easier to blame an app than himself for any failure. She quelled the impulse to grasp Pocock's shoulders and shake him; if her father were still chief, he wouldn't be able to sleep at night with a hurricane bearing down. "Of course, any off-islanders here for overnight stays in the Basin won't get those warnings. We should assume a number of itinerant boat owners may be blindsided and trapped."

"I'll make a note to offer our support to the Coast Guard." Pocock's barely controlled boredom meant he was tired of Merry, but she figured the stakes were too high to let him balls-up disaster response.

"And of course, right now," she plowed on, "we can help the situation a *ton* just by directing traffic on Washington Street and other pinch points—Children's Beach is a biggie—where boat trailers will snarl intersections. It's going to be chaos in Madaket, too, once people start fighting for ramp space to haul their vessels out of the water."

"Right." Pocock's mouth furled in a snarl. He had often told Merry that Nantucket's ban on traffic lights was ridiculous, because it forced *people* to manage a simple problem of urban order. Washington Street's gridlock was a personal wound.

"NEMA will take care of setting up a shelter at the high school, and distributing relief supplies from the elementary school," she concluded hurriedly, before he could launch into his favorite diatribe, "but they'll need police at both places, for security."

NEMA was the Nantucket Emergency Management

Agency, an island-sized version of the federal one that coordinated disaster relief.

Pocock sighed and glanced at his watch. "That meeting's now in fifteen minutes."

"Yes, sir."

He paused, teeth working at his lower lip. "I'm designating you notetaker."

"Very well, sir." Merry felt a surge of relief. At least she'd know where the gaps and problems were, heading into the storm.

"You'll get your notes—and any resulting suggestions—to Scott Tredlow."

"Of course, sir."

From long habit, Merry waited for Pocock's final word before turning to the door. This time, she counted to twenty-three while he tapped his keyboard.

"And detective?" he finally said. "Wedding or no? If disaster hits, you're on call, just like the rest of us."

In Provincetown, he underestimated her.

"Let's go dancing tonight," she said playfully, catching Matt's wrist and swinging him around. "I brought a sundress I haven't had a chance to wear."

They walked from the marina up to Commercial Street, Matt and Ashley holding hands. He was third wheel again, following a few paces behind, his eyes trained on the shop windows and tourists cycling through the dusk. They followed the sound of a DJ into The Underground, where a few bodies wavered on the dance floor. He drifted toward a pool table. Matt ordered drinks. He turned his back on their whispers, the sudden shot of Ashley's laughter. He was simmering with jealousy and longing he could neither dispel nor deny. Vodka helped a bit. So did the sound of balls clicking into pockets. The combination must have lulled his brain because when Matt touched his shoulder, he was surprised to find him alone.

"She's gone," Matt said tightly.

"What do you mean?"

"She went to the bathroom and hasn't come back. What does she know? What have you told her?"

He shook his head, his mind racing. "Nothing. I swear."

"What does she suspect?"

Everything. "Matt—"

"Come on."

"You're not going to find her!"

Matt turned his head, already at the door. "She'll go back to the boat. She won't leave all her stuff. That's a rookie mistake—needing things too much."

He was right, of course.

They caught up with Ash, heading the wrong way on the pier, canvas tote on her shoulder and suitcase behind her. Her cell phone was in her hand; she'd probably called a car service. He hoped she hadn't called the police.

Ashley stopped short when she saw them. Stepped back a fraction, calculating her chances.

"I want to go home," she said. Her voice was as plaintive as a tired toddler's, worn out by fun. "I need to go back to work."

"That's not possible." Matt slipped her phone out of her hand and tossed it into the water. Ashley made a faint mew of protest. But she didn't try to go after it.

Matt smiled down into her eyes, gentle as death. Just as he had that first day in Long Island, when the sun still shone and only a fool would pass on adventure.

His hands circled her throat. From a distance, it probably looked like love.

Chapter Three

TUESDAY MORNING, PETER pulled his Range Rover to a halt in front of the Mason Farms barn and found two young women in hoodies shivering beside his foreman, Rafe da Silva. Once the hurricane forecast had broken the day before, Rafe had hired a couple of construction guys to board up the farmhouse's windows and reinforce the barn doors as much as possible. The sound of hammers and an electric saw filtered through the air now; steel ladders were propped against Peter's second story. He glanced inquiringly at Rafe and the two women as he got out of the car.

"Pete, this is Brittany, and this is her sister, Cara." Rafe gestured toward the pair. "They usually work with Tess at the Greengage, but I thought they could help us hunt sheep."

The Greengage was Tess da Silva's acclaimed restaurant downtown, the base from which she planned to cater Peter's wedding at the end of the week, if anything was still standing once the hurricane passed.

"That's great." Peter offered his hand to each of the women. "I appreciate your help. We need to get our flock of merinos off the moors and into the shearing barn, but we have to find them all first. Sheep tend to stray, and they've got fifty acres to hide in."

Cara glanced at the massive farm building beyond the house. "Is that the shearing barn?"

Peter shook his head. "You can't see it from here. This barn is for equipment and offices."

"With living quarters overhead," Rafe added. "I'll be sleeping there the next few nights."

Peter's brows rose in surprise.

"Somebody's got to watch this place," his foreman said. "You're getting married."

"Congratulations, by the way." Brittany grinned at Peter. "We're also your wedding staff. So, good with lamb—on the hoof, or off."

"Thanks," Peter said, and meant it. He turned and threw open the car's tailgate. Ney, his mixed-breed herding dog, leapt out and pawed happily at Rafe's knees.

"Sheep don't stand a chance now," Rafe said, tousling Ney's ears fondly. "Let's load up."

Mason Farms covered a hundred acres in the middle of the moors at the south end of the island, not far from a local landmark called Altar Rock. A stone's throw to the northeast was Gibbs Pond, a freshwater remnant of the last ice age. Peter knew that if hurricane winds drove the Atlantic inland, the pond and then his bogs would overflow with brackish water. His crop would be ruined by salt. As Rafe drove along the causeway between the bogs toward the sheep pasture beyond, Peter ran his eyes over the cranberry vines, heavy with red fruit.

"We could wet harvest some of it," he said.

"Waste of good cranberries," the foreman replied. Wet harvesting bruised the fruit more than dry-harvesting, and bruised berries fetched a lower price. Bruised berries were used for juice, dry-harvested for the grocery shelves.

Wet-harvesting was faster—but it took time, care, and manpower. The bogs had to be flooded with water, then stimulated with pumps that gently dislodged the berries from the vines. Booms were unfurled and floated on the bog surface to corral the berries, while teams of harvesters in bright rubber waders swished through the flooded bog, skimming the fruit and placing it on conveyer belts that carried it to truck beds. Load after load of perfect cranberries took weeks and crew and extra equipment to harvest. Extra equipment Peter had already reserved on the mainland, intending to ship it over to Nantucket in mid-October. He usually started harvesting in late September, it was true—but this year, he'd been waiting until after his honeymoon.

When his crop could already be trashed.

"Let's get the sheep into the shearing barn while we can," Rafe said, "and worry about the bog tomorrow."

In the face of a hurricane, Peter knew, saving his flock would have to be enough.

"I'M NOT CONCERNED about Ted Whittaker," Jack mused as he and Dionis humped over the sandy Tuckernuck trail in his battered spare truck Tuesday afternoon. As far as the eye could see, the surrounding moors rolled unevenly to the horizon, a map of color as their vegetation flamed with autumn. Huge flocks of gulls and terns, storm petrels and shearwaters, filled the air with raucous insults and reprisals. On the horizon, Dionis glimpsed only a bank of gray cloud and a wavering line of surf—no homes in this direction that she could see, and no human life. Tuckernuck was the emptiest place she knew, the most wildly beautiful, and the loneliest. Particularly at night. Dark as ink, once the sun went down, and vaulted with stars.

"Ted's already got the Whaler out of North Pond and stored in the garage of the main house," Jack continued. "Hired Will Sadler to help board up his windows. The guy listens to his radio. Says he'll be ready to leave the island tomorrow. I'm putting him and Will on the noon boat."

Dionis liked Ted Whittaker. He was roughly her father's age—early sixties—a history professor who lived during the winter in a town north of Boston. Ted talked books whenever he ran into her, usually local author Nathaniel Philbrick's, which Dionis devoured as soon as they hit the shelves. The first Whittakers had arrived on Tuckernuck sometime in the 1920s—not as deep-rooted a family as the Cabotts, but close enough. Ted was raising his grandchildren to love Tuck as much as he did. They would inherit the compound on North Pond one day—a main house and three shingled cottages sprinkled over some ten acres.

"You left a flyer at China Trade?" Jack asked as they turned left at a fork in the road and bucketed toward the next property, a 1950s Dutch Colonial in worse condition than either of them liked. Dionis had distributed her printed notices the previous day while Jack screwed plywood sheets to the window frames of empty houses.

"Yeah," Dionis said. "Elsa was probably out working when I drove by. And Brad—" She didn't need to finish the sentence. Jack knew all about Elsa Chamberlain's boyfriend. He was supposed to be writing a book. It would have been nice, Dionis reflected, if Brad Kramer had spent some of his considerable spare time tacking shingles back onto China Trade's roof. Too late, now.

Elsa Chamberlain was a professional photographer based in Providence. She could get lost for hours in the Tuckernuck landscape, capturing weather and clouds and sea and wildlife in endlessly varied combinations. She taught at the Rhode Island School of Design during the winter, but she and Brad lived completely off the grid on Tuck during the summer months. Elsa had inherited China Trade unexpectedly from a childless uncle.

"She told me in May she wanted to get some work done on the place," Jack muttered, "but then never scheduled it. Can't do work for free, Di, but hell—I feel bad for Elsa now. This house is going to sustain some damage." He honked the truck horn as he rolled up to China Trade's front door. It stood ajar, a screen shielding the entrance. Somebody was home, then.

Dionis lowered her window and called out, "Hello?"

There was no response.

Jack hit his horn again. Dionis shoved open her truck door and stepped down onto the springy grass that ran straight up to the granite threshold.

"Hello? *Elsa*? Brad?"

There was the sound of shattering glass from somewhere inside the house, and an explosive expletive, quickly stifled.

The screen door swung open. Brad: bare-chested, blond, with handsomely burnished skin and a gold signet on his right pinky finger. His jeans were artfully torn and his strong feet were bare. A tattoo of an octopus rolled across his six-pack abs. *He's a walking ad for sex*, Dionis marveled. A half-empty handle of bourbon dangled from Brad's left hand. It was only one-twenty in the afternoon; Dionis guessed he'd started drinking before noon. Most of the trash the Mathers carted away from China Trade was empty bottles.

"Hey, guys," Brad said. "What's up?"

"Is Elsa around?" Dionis called.

"Out back. In the darkroom." Brad glanced behind him vaguely. "We got your garbage here *somewhere.*"

"Great!" Dionis managed. "Did you get our note yesterday? . . . About the hurricane?"

Brad took a swig from the bourbon bottle and shook his head. "What hurricane?"

"The one that's supposed to hit tomorrow night. We're evacuating everyone from Tuck today and tomorrow."

Brad swayed slightly in China Trade's doorway.

"Di," her father murmured, low enough that Brad couldn't hear, "just walk around to the darkroom, will you, and tell Elsa?"

"*Shit.* Tell Elsa!" Brad groaned, flapping his free hand.

"I'll do that." Released, Dionis headed for the side of the house. Jack had built Elsa Chamberlain's free-standing darkroom in China Trade's backyard three summers before. It had no windows to board up or shatter, and was the only structure on the property sturdy enough to weather a major storm. Elsa had found the money to pay for what really mattered to her.

Caretakers, Dionis reflected as she ran toward the darkroom, knew way too much.

"There's weather coming," he told Ash as he dropped down the gangway from the flybridge onto the main deck.

She was reading a paperback in the comfortable lounge area, and made a point of ignoring him. She'd said little to either of them since they'd frog-marched her back to Shytown. As though if she couldn't scream or run, she didn't have to exist for them in this moment either.

"Ash," he said urgently, "you've got to listen. The storm could be serious, and Matt won't risk going into port. He's afraid you'll try to leave."

Her lips curved slightly, a secret pleasure. "Party's got to end sometime."

"Matt thinks he can outrun a hurricane." He grasped her shoulders, willing her to look at him. She flinched, and redoubled her focus on the book. But her whole body had stiffened, as though she were waiting for a blow.

Filled with self-hatred, he released her.

"Ash. When the storm hits, stay close to me."

Finally, she lifted her eyes. Finally, he knew she was listening.

"Anything can happen in a hurricane," he said. "Anyone can go overboard."

"Even Matt?" she asked.

And gave him that same secret smile.

Chapter Four

"PETER!"

He stepped into the comforting glow of the hallway after nine hours of heavy labor, closing the front door of the Cliff Road house firmly behind him to shut out the gusting wind. For a second, he thought he was hearing things. "George?"

And there she was—his sister, with her shining cap of dark hair and her expressive hands, moving like a whirlwind from her perch on the sofa to throw her arms around him.

"You came early!" he crowed.

"I'm not stubborn, like our mother," she retorted, stepping back to study his face. "I want to *be* here to see you get married—and by Thursday, planes and ferries could be canceled. I changed all our flights yesterday and pulled the kids out of school. They're ecstatic. How are you? Nervous? Excited?"

"Exhausted," he said. "It's a bitch trying to secure a cranberry bog from a hurricane." He and Rafe had managed to find the last stray sheep by two o'clock that afternoon, then spent the remaining hours of daylight flooding the bog so they could wet-harvest cranberries. A partially filled container truckload of fruit now sat securely in the main barn. If the weather allowed, they'd harvest some more tomorrow. *Small victories*, Peter thought.

"This storm's timing is dreadful," Georgiana murmured sympathetically. "You have help at the farm, yes?"

"I do." There was no point in trying to explain how he'd spent the past few days; Georgiana managed four children's complex lives and schedules. She was the master of her own multitasking and had no sympathy to spare for other people's.

"Hey, Uncle Pete," Trey Whitney called out from the kitchen. Trey was the eldest of George's four kids, a freshman in high school, far too cool to hug Peter. He wore shorts and an Emirates soccer jersey and appeared not to have cut his hair since they'd last met in August. A fistful of chips and a container of salsa were clutched in Trey's hands. "Merry's ordered pizza for dinner!"

I'm sure she has, Peter thought with sudden amusement. Arriving home from work to find six more people in the Cliff Road house, Merry would have scrambled on the food front. George had clearly forgotten to telegraph the change in the Whitney travel plans before she landed on Nantucket. Peter wondered if there were any sheets on the guest beds yet. *Never mind*, he chided himself. George knew where everything was kept; she spent six weeks in the house every summer. Maybe she'd even get the kids to make their own beds, in exchange for the extra days off from school.

"I'm so glad you're here," he said, throwing his arm around his sister. "It feels like a party. I take it Mother refused to change flights?"

"Of course." George squeezed his waist and led him toward the kitchen. "I tried to persuade her. A full ten minutes on the phone. She's balking at paying change fees, if you can believe. Sniffed about how tiresome it is to be forced to fly *commercial*. Come say hello to Hale. He's opening a bottle of something red that goes with pizza."

"I GOT THE Radleigh boys to help us tomorrow after school," Jack told Dionis as she joined him in the kitchen.

Ryan and Jake Radleigh, sixteen and eighteen, were native Nantucketers and the Mathers' summer help.

"Tell them to skip school entirely," she suggested, accepting a bowl of Jack's beef stew. "They can board up windows while we transport people."

Dionis had showered and changed and her hair was freshly washed; her tired muscles ached less now that she'd run gallons of scalding water over them. She sat down at the table, famished and grateful for the shared house and her father's cooking.

"We've got sixteen folks, by my count, to ferry over here tomorrow." Jack took his usual chair across the table. "If you handle one skiff and I take the other, we should be able to get everybody and their luggage off by early afternoon."

Spoon in hand, Dionis did a mental headcount. Seven Tuckernuck houses still had people in them, and Jack was right—the total number to evacuate was about sixteen. The skiffs could each handle four or five passengers with all their luggage. Round trip between Madaket and Tuckernuck would take an hour, with rising surf.

"We can head back in the afternoon, if the weather holds, with another load of plywood," her father persisted, "and finish the windows as long as the daylight lasts. Current landfall forecast is late tomorrow night, early hours of Thursday. But the location has shifted north. It's headed straight for us, and it'll be a Cat Three when it arrives."

She choked on a lump of beef and stared at him, struggling to clear her throat. *Cat Three.* Insane winds and huge storm surge and damage to every bit of housing all over the island—nobody would escape, nobody would be safe. There were only degrees of danger now. Anxiety washed from the back of her neck to her groin in a warm wave.

"The rain will start by morning." Jack shoved his bowl away distractedly, his mind elsewhere. Then he rubbed his left bicep again. He had been up on three different roofs with power tools and a hammer that afternoon.

"Do you want some ice for your arm?" Dionis asked.

"Nah. I'm just out of ibuprofen."

"I'll run to The Rotary and get you some."

"It'll pass," he said irritably. He hated her fussing. "Relax. You've done enough today."

God knows that was true. But a Cat Three? Dionis carried their bowls to the sink and ran some water into them. *We're responsible. For all of it.* "What about Northern Light? Is anyone still out there?"

"How would we know?" he joked. "Not like they're paying us to keep tabs on them. We're too low-rent, Di."

Northern Light was Tuckernuck's showplace, shockingly new. It commanded twenty acres and eleven thousand square feet. Seven bathrooms, a wine cellar, and personal gym. A media room and restaurant-grade kitchen; three terraces for entertaining; a swimming pool fed with saltwater, piped up from the ocean. A three-bedroom guest cottage. A helipad, and a horse barn tucked up against the solar array that powered the place.

Nothing like it had ever been seen on Tuckernuck, and the owners didn't mix with anybody else on the island. Todd Benson was a star NFL quarterback. He and his supermodel wife, Bianca, flew in their friends and staff on helicopters when they wanted to party.

Northern Light had an electronic gate across its quahog shell drive—the only graded driveway on Tuckernuck. Dionis hadn't been able to get near the door with her flyer yesterday. She and Jack weren't the estate's caretakers; the Bensons hired their own people for maintenance. They owned their own powerboat, too, and ran it back and forth to Nantucket's restaurants and clubs at will. But it was Jack who'd brought the Bensons' two palominos, Honeybear and Afterglow, across Madaket Sound on his barge the previous June. Bianca Benson liked to ride bareback along the sand in a bikini. Todd liked to photograph her while she rode. Jack and Dionis had met the horse trailer and groom at Jackson Point and delivered them safely to the electronic gate.

Dionis hadn't seen any of them since.

"I hate those dicks," she said now.

"Di." Jack's voice disapproved.

"They have no sense of history. No idea where Tuckernuck comes from, or why it's precious. They just want to gut the place for their own pleasure."

"I left a message about the hurricane with Todd Benson's personal assistant in New York." Jack lifted his hands in a gesture of helplessness. "It's the only contact number I've got."

"And?"

"She texted me back. Said it was all good—the Bensons have no plans to fly in this weekend."

"What about the horses?" Dionis demanded. "And that woman who takes care of them?" What was the groom's name—Mandy? Maddie?

"Must've hired some other barge to float them off," Jack said carelessly. "Certainly didn't hire mine."

"*Dicks*." Dionis paused. "So—not our circus, not our monkeys?"

"Exactly," her father replied.

HOWIE SEITZ CHANGED into jeans and a Cisco Brewers T-shirt before heading to Stop & Shop that evening. Over the past two days he'd felt the hurricane turn its head slowly and bear down on Nantucket as unswervingly as a heat-seeking missile, sweeping everything from its path. He had gone from door to door through half-deserted neighborhoods, ordering the holdouts to evacuate as soon as possible, and directed traffic for hours in front of the Town Pier, where boat owners were still hauling vessels out of the harbor. He'd stacked walls of sandbags around the diesel substation that would probably be inundated within hours. Taken last-minute first-aid training at the fire station, with an emphasis on CPR. Set up cots in the high school gymnasium, and blocked off all the parking areas that were sure to flood on New Whale and Water Streets.

He was yawning his head off now and wanted nothing more than to sack out in front of his TV. But tonight, along with the rest of the island, Howie needed to buy bottled water, batteries, beer, and sandwich meat. That and a few bags of chips should get him through the duration. He circled the Stop & Shop parking lot for ten minutes before finding a parking space for his battered Nissan. Everyone was hunting groceries before Nantucket's roads were too flooded to navigate.

Howie lived in a one-bedroom apartment over a garage off New Mill Street, not far from the Quaker cemetery— a caretaker's quarters, behind a summer home that was currently empty. The owners figured an off duty cop made a great tenant. He had only three windows, but hadn't had enough time or daylight to board them up yet. *Maybe tomorrow*, he thought. If there was any plywood left at Marine Home.

He'd parked his shopping cart in front of the market's deli counter and was checking his cell phone, one hand in the pocket of his jeans, when somebody touched his shoulder. He turned and stared straight into Dionis Mather's dark blue eyes.

"Nice haircut," she said lightly. "I wasn't sure it was you."

"Hey, Di." He tucked his phone away, feeling heat rise suddenly to his chest and linger there. *You look tired*, he wanted to blurt out. *Are you sleeping okay?* But he said only, "How you doing?"

"Fine. You?"

"Fine, I guess." He shrugged. *Lonely, actually. Pissed as hell, to be frank. Still wondering why you ghosted me.* Overhead, the supermarket lights swayed, and acoustic ceiling tiles lifted in a sudden gust of wind. Howie and Dionis both looked up.

"Man. Weather's crazy, right?" he said.

"Yeah." She met his eyes. "This is, like, the twelfth time I've been here for supplies in the past thirty-six hours—when I'm not out in the middle of Madaket. Wind's already hitting thirty knots on the water. Skiff's getting harder to control."

Howie understood, suddenly. "You and Jack tying down Tuck's loose ends?"

"We've gone through a lot of hammers and nails. Boarding up windows and sliding glass doors. Tomorrow, we have to get the last few clients off. And cross our fingers." She held up her palms, which were swollen and red. "Mine are shot from lifting plywood."

Howie took her right hand in his and gently smoothed the palm. "Wish I could help you."

Dionis drew her hand away. "I'm sure you're just as slammed."

He laughed, harshly. "I spent the day being ordered around by a buddy. Scott Tredlow. He's the PD's emergency management coordinator—and man, does he like to coordinate."

"I know Scott." Dionis mustered a smile. "He called my dad to ask who was left out on Tuckernuck. We told him we had it handled."

"Remember his name, in case you don't."

"I will—if things go to hell, and I need help."

Howie was about to tell her that the only name and help she would ever really need is his, if only she'd see it, but said instead, "Get those last folks off as soon as possible. This storm's path is looking pretty unpredictable. First, they were saying landfall would be Rhode Island, now they're saying they've got no idea, but it could hit here and by then it'll be a Cat Three. The Coast Guard issued a small-craft warning this afternoon—"

"You think I don't know that?" Dionis interrupted. "I

listen to the NOAA weather band and Channel Twelve all day, Howie." Channel 12 was the Coast Guard's VHF frequency for marine broadcasts. A wave of irritation and weariness swept over Dionis's face. She rubbed her forehead, her gaze dropping. "Sorry. I'm just tired. And to think I wasted years getting a master's in history. I could be teaching AP European at Exeter right now."

Howie bit back a few words. He knew all about Dionis's dreams. And how much it cost her to postpone them.

"Anyway, I just ran in for ibuprofen," she added lamely. "Jack's pulled a muscle or something. His left arm hurts so bad he's having trouble lifting it."

"That can't be good. If he can't hold onto you, how's he going to keep you in line?"

Dionis smiled faintly. "I seem to be the only one who's worried. Jack's a stoic, you know that."

Howie hesitated, then thought, *Fuck it*. He had nothing more to lose.

"I'm done here, Di. But I was going to stop by Lola's." He brushed her shoulder tentatively. "Come with me. You look like you could use a drink."

"You lied about tracking the storm," Matt shouted at him. "Or maybe you just blew the navigation. Which is it?"

"Falmouth," he said desperately. It was vital to focus on what they needed to survive, not this fool's anger. "Falmouth. We can still get there in time."

Matt shook his head. "I'm not pulling into any port on the Cape. What if the bitch called 911 in P-town before we caught up with her? They'll be looking for us."

"You're crazy." He turned furiously toward the gangway, finished with pleas and blame, but Matt moved faster, blocking his path. There was a gun in Matt's hand.

He stared in disbelief at the Glock—all that blunt force ignorance.

The safety was off.

Where was Ashley?

"We've got one more meeting marked there on your charts," Matt said. "Oak Bluffs."

"No! It's not worth the risk!"

A furious gust of wind hit Shytown's flybridge, almost carrying it away.

Matt grinned and pressed the muzzle against his diaphragm. "Get us there."

Chapter Five

THAT WEDNESDAY MORNING, Merry pulled her
police SUV halfway onto the brick sidewalk of narrow Fair Street, a few feet from the entrance of Tattle
Court, and left the hazard lights flashing. The sky was
gray, and the faintest mist—not quite fog, not quite rain,
but something her father called *soft Irish weather*—had
blanketed Nantucket overnight. Against the backdrop
of houses uniformly clad in charcoal-colored shingles,
the mist leached all life from landscape and sea. The
island and everything it contained was monochrome
and dripping.

Tattle Court's neighbors would neither notice nor
worry to find a police cruiser nearly blocking their access;
for nearly sixty years, two chiefs of the Nantucket Police
in succession had lived on this cul-de-sac off Fair Street.
Merry hurried around to the rear of her family home and
nearly tripped over a storm cellar door, flung wide on the
unmown grass.

She clutched at the side of the house to keep from pitching into the cellar's darkness. A snow-white head bobbed
slowly upwards through the opening as Ralph Waldo
Folger climbed deliberately to ground level, then swiveled in surprise as he caught sight of his granddaughter's

trousered leg. She was massaging it painfully with her free hand.

"Meredith Abiah!" he exclaimed. "What are you doing in uniform?"

"Pocock has all hands on deck," she explained. "I'm not working a case at the moment, so I get to cruise the 'Sconset Bluff and tell any homeowners still out there that they ought to evacuate." The Bluff had been eroding for decades, despite the most ingenious efforts at recapturing its beaches' sand. More than one multimillion-dollar place would fall into the sea by week's end.

Merry grasped Ralph's hand. With a grunt, he hoisted himself upright from the final cellar step. "What were you doing down there?"

"Sweeping it out and making it comfortable," her grandfather said. "Shoved all the fishing gear and Christmas decorations aside, and set up a couple of deck chairs, blankets, a propane stove for coffee and baked beans, and a shortwave radio for your father and me. Worked well in '91, so why change a thing?"

"Have you got bottled water? Flashlights and batteries?"

Ralph shrugged. "I prefer beer. Hundred-year-old oil lamps last longer than flashlights, and cast more light. How about you, Meredith? Has Young Peter got that roof walk tied down tight? You're a tad exposed on Cliff Road."

"Oh, the house'll be fine." She helped Ralph heave shut the heavy cellar doors and secure their iron hasps. "It's everything else that's gone to hell in a handbasket."

Her grandfather quirked a ferocious eyebrow. "I had no idea women your age are familiar with that phrase. It's archaic."

"Yeah, well, I was raised in isolation."

"Is the wedding off?"

"It's profoundly rearranged."

"But everything is *well*, between yourself and Peter?"

"Of course, Ralph," Merry said impatiently. "We're too crazed with storm prep to get cold feet or last-minute nerves. The tent people arrived this morning to pull up all the poles they'd carefully planted Monday—and refunded our deposit. The florist called to explain I had a choice: accept a bouquet of whatever she has on hand, which will probably be wilted by Saturday—or carry silk flowers."

"No shipments with the ferries canceled the next few days, of course," Ralph sighed. "But your dress is done! And the food will be excellent!"

"Even there, we may have a problem." Merry glowered. "No tent means *no tables*. No space for a sit-down dinner. Eighty-three people are coming, Ralph. I'm meeting with Tess da Silva right now, on the way to work, to see if she can turn her entire menu into finger food. We'll be balancing plates on the arm of a sofa."

"It'll be lovely," Ralph Waldo soothed. He reached out and gathered Merry close, kissing her temple. "The church will still be standing—as it has for three hundred years. Peter will be standing, too, right next to you. If we all get our feet damp walking back to the Cliff Road house—so much the merrier."

"No dance floor," Merry mourned. She had resisted the whole notion of one six months ago, but lately the idea of whirling around on Ralph's arm under the stars had grown on her.

"Then I'll waltz you down the middle of the table, dear heart."

Her cell phone rang. She pulled it out of her pocket. "Hello, George?"

Ralph waited patiently. But the conversation was brief.

"That was Peter's sister," Merry explained, as she stabbed the call to silence. "His mother is grounded in Manhattan. She sends all of us her regrets."

THE DRINK AT Lola's had turned into two: bourbon for Howie and wine for Dionis. The quick detour had stretched past an hour, then an hour and a half—as the wind tugged at the bar's roof and Howie told her stories that made her laugh. The nagging regret she'd felt since she'd dumped him had fled, replaced with giddy happiness. Howie was still there. Howie still cared.

She'd stopped returning his calls weeks ago—somewhere in the middle of the August caretaking craziness. But as her father drove her out to Madaket this morning, Dionis stopped lying to herself. She hadn't dumped Howie because of work. She could name the exact day and minute she'd decided he was dangerous. And better cut out of her life.

She'd been loading bag after bag of someone else's groceries into the belly of her work skiff: a flat of fresh strawberries, fresh baguettes of bread, a case of white wine and a case of red. Filet mignon, shitake mushrooms, and pounds of fresh tomatoes; corn and lettuce she'd picked up at Bartlett's Farm. Logs of goat cheese. Expensive flatbread crackers imported from England. Harpooned swordfish steaks from 167 Raw, and containers of Straightwarf's bluefish pâté. Bottles of artisanal tonic and small-batch gin. Warm Scotch-Irish cake and doughnuts from the Downyflake.

And she had thought to herself: *I can't go on like this.* It wasn't the disparity between the menu she was delivering and the one that sustained her at home, or the fact that so much luxury seemed vital to these clients living beyond civilization. It wasn't a conviction born of class resentment. Dionis had grown up on Nantucket—she understood that it thrived because of seasonal money and the folks who served it. The backbreaking work of every summer, the runs across the roiling green chop of Madaket Harbor, the sun on her tanned back, and her long hair pulled like a rope through the eyelet of a fisherman's cap, had felt carefree when she was eighteen. They'd felt like freedom. But she was nearly thirty now, and she wanted more from her life.

She wanted to move to the mainland. Find a teaching job, and use her degree. Write a book, maybe, in her free time—

Howie would prevent all that.

Because it was as she was lifting the flat of strawberries, and the smoky-sweet scent of ripeness flooded her nose, that Dionis closed her eyes and saw Howie's face. He was feeding her a strawberry, one late morning in bed, his gaze fixed on her mouth with an intensity that sent fingers up and down Di's spine. She craved Howie on her tongue.

I'm in love with him, she'd thought. And, horrified, she'd dropped the entire flat of strawberries all over the skiff's floor.

She couldn't let Howie hold her back. He loved everything about Nantucket and his job, and he intended to stay forever. He'd told Dionis that. Their dreams did not align.

Never mind, she thought now as Jack pulled their truck

into the Jackson Point lot and killed the engine. *Never mind that I kissed him when we left Lola's last night. I won't let it happen again.*

THE RADLEIGH BOYS had skipped school and were waiting for them, hoodies pulled tight over their ears and hands stuffed in their jeans, at the end of the boat landing. Madaket Harbor was steel gray under a lowering sky, Dionis saw, and the wind that had kicked up overnight was blowing in gale-force gusts. Well above yesterday's thirty knots, she suspected. She hunched her shoulders against it, eyes scanning the horizon. Tuckernuck's outline was impossible to discern in the aqueous light.

"Jake, you come with me, and Ryan, you go with Di," Jack told the boys. Ryan was the elder of the two; he immediately jumped into Di's skiff and started the engine. He was a good kid. His dad taught history at the high school. Dionis had bumped into all of them at Nantucket Bookworks in the off-season, buying paperbacks of classics Mark Radleigh wanted his boys to read. Dionis had noticed how Ryan and Jake held the books as delicately as butterflies, as though a binding and paper were alien in their digital hands.

She waited for Jack to lead the way out of the harbor and guided her skiff after his. Then she let Ryan take the skiff's helm and slipped back into thoughts of Howie. When his arms encircled her, Dionis felt safe. Felt the profoundest sensation of *home.* Impossible to talk to Ryan, anyway, with the competing roars of engine and wind. Her father would tell Ry what to do once they reached land. The skiff bucketed over the increasing chop, and Dionis grasped the gunwales firmly as she sat amidships.

MERRY FOUND TESS Starbuck da Silva alone in the kitchen of the Greengage, the restaurant she owned on a quiet side street not far from the Folger family home. Tess had raised her son, Will, in the neatly shingled house she'd inherited from her late husband. But when Will left for college in Boston—he was now a sophomore—she'd opened up the entire main floor for dining, and upgraded her kitchen to gleaming commercial standards. Tess and her second husband, Rafe, no longer lived above the restaurant; during the tourist season, the Greengage's hours ran too late and its clientele were too noisy. As foreman of Mason Farms, Rafe was early to bed, early to rise. He and Tess now owned a diminutive saltbox on the Polpis Road, and met halfway between their work lives each night.

"I've got a backup generator here," Tess was saying as she handed Merry a cup of coffee, "so my burners and ovens should work, regardless. I can't believe you don't have a generator on Cliff Road."

"Nobody lives there off-season," Merry pointed out, "when a backup is usually needed. Peter has a number out at the farm, of course."

"Which is why I asked Rafe to bring one over to the house." Tess smirked. "He thought the sheep needed light and heat more than you did. I told him not to argue."

"That'll be great, Tess," Merry said with relief. "Even if the main power goes out, George's kids will still be able to charge their laptops and cell phones. I was dreading life with a bunch of media-starved teenagers."

"Tell George to expect my girls today," Tess warned. "Cara and Brittany. I'm sending them over before the deluge with glasses, linens, and plates."

"You can still pull off a feast, then?" Merry asked, worried. "Without a tent or tables?"

"I can." Tess hugged her. "My kitchen didn't meet commercial code for years. I was cooking out of a shoebox. And strangely enough, the local police never turned me in. I owe you my best on your wedding day, Mer—and that's what you'll get."

"THE CONDITION OF these roads is a disgrace," Honoria Cabott declared as Jack's truck rocked over the ruts leading from Vineyard View to the unpaved track heading south and east to Tuckernuck's cove. She was sitting in the passenger seat of the cab, her fingers clutching the armrest. "Don't you people *grade* anymore?"

"Dad brings a grader over in May," Dionis told her. "It's just the end of the season now, Miss Cabott—and there's no point in doing the roads again until the winter's passed."

"I don't know what we pay for," Honoria said fretfully.

She was nervous, Dionis knew, about leaving her home and returning to the assisted living facility. Nervous, perhaps, about crossing the sea in gale-force winds. Honoria weighed less than a hundred pounds and looked ready to take flight when she was sitting on her own porch. Perched in the exposed body of the work skiff, she'd be tossed overboard if they weren't careful.

When they reached the cove, Dionis helped the frail woman out of the truck and watched Jorie guide her carefully down the dock to the steel gantry. Ted Whittaker was already loading his luggage into Jack's work skiff. His golden retriever, Barney, was at the skiff's stern, wearing a bright red canine life jacket.

"Take Jake with you," Dionis suggested to her father—the younger Radleigh boy played defense on the Whalers' lacrosse team and his bulk was excellent ballast—"and seat him next to Miss Cabott, to buffer her from the swell. He can help you with the luggage in Madaket."

"I'll put Jorie on her other side," Jack agreed. "That's all we can do, short of tying Miss Cabott down."

"She'd bite your hands off before you even got close."

But her father was no longer listening to her. He was squinting at something over Dionis's shoulder, a puzzled expression on his face. She turned, and glimpsed a young woman in jeans and a short down jacket hurrying toward them, a duffel bag over her shoulder and a large suitcase rolling disjointedly over the sand. Dionis narrowed her eyes to make out the face—she couldn't place it. About her own age, with a mane of strawberry-blonde hair coiled in a knot.

"Who the hell is she? And how did we miss her over the past three days?"

Her father sighed heavily. "*Oh my Gawd.* That's the woman who works at Northern Light. Mandy. Maddie? You know—takes care of the Benson horses?"

Dionis swore. The Bensons *hadn't* handled their own hurricane prep. If the groom was still on Tuckernuck, so were Honeybear and Afterglow, the Bensons' palominos.

The woman raised an arm in the air and waved at them frantically. "Hey! You *guys!* Wait for me!"

It took Dionis several trips from the truck to the skiff to transfer Vineyard View's luggage. Jorie Engstrom was a weaver in her spare time; she'd brought a large hand loom on a collapsible stand and all her wool supplies to Tuckernuck for the protracted stay between May and October. Miss Cabott left nothing behind in the Assisted Living facility when she departed—"those crones will steal everything not nailed down"—and her entire worldly goods were returning, now, to Madaket. By the time they were loaded and the Vineyard View pair had joined Ted Whittaker in the skiff, Jack was walking away from the Northern Light stranger with a troubled expression on his face.

"She left the horses behind," he told Dionis.

"So—the circus, and all its monkeys, are dumped now in our laps?"

"She says Todd Benson was supposed to call. About the arrangements." Jack pursed his lips. "She was shocked he hadn't. Walked all the way here, too, from Northern Light, when she realized we were evacuating Tuck."

"My heart bleeds. What about the Palominos?"

"They're loose in the paddock. So they can graze."

"In other words, completely vulnerable to a Category Three hurricane."

Jack looked at Dionis helplessly.

"You are *not* going to run that woman back to Madaket, Dad," she protested. "We have a schedule. *Priorities.*"

"There's not much time, Di, to dick around with this. If we leave her here now—and the storm hits . . . are we certain we can get back out to save her?" Jack halted. "Hey, *Ryan*—take a golf cart and head to China Trade. Make sure Ms. Chamberlain and Brad are awake. Tell 'em Di is coming along behind to load 'em up."

Dionis snorted. "Does that woman really think she can just leave two palominos alone in a field in a hurricane? Does *Todd Benson* think so?"

"I'm sure they have access to the barn."

"That can't be good enough. Not with the whole world blowing into the stalls at a hundred and twenty miles an hour." Dionis knew next to nothing about horses, but she figured they felt nervous in bad weather.

Jack shrugged. "I can't get cell coverage here, Di. I'll call Benson's assistant when I get back to Madaket, see what he wants to do."

"Dad." She fought back her impatience. "Nothing but a barge will float off a pair of horses. And we can't use our barge today."

The Mathers' barge hauled everything massive—like a fully loaded horse trailer—to and from Tuckernuck, but it was moored at Madaket Marine, on Hither Creek, near the powerboat required to tow it. Even with the Radleigh boys' help, it would take hours to mobilize that kind of multi-vessel transport operation—and today, at this hour and with terrific wind gusts and increasingly rising seas, a barge could founder. Horses and all.

"I know. *Dammit.*"

Dionis marched purposefully over to the Benson groom, who was shifting her luggage to the end of the dock's steel gantry. She would probably coil the mooring painter around her neck rather than be left behind, Dionis thought, if they refused to take her.

"Maddie?"

"It's Mandy, actually." She lifted her head but failed to meet Di's eyes; not as old or as confident as she'd like to suggest. A few years younger than Di, in fact. Without Di's toughness.

"Great. I'm Dionis," she said. "My dad and I can't possibly get the Bensons' horses off Tuckernuck today.

You need to stay with them until we've got a plan in place."

Mandy glanced at her watch. "My plane leaves in three hours. How long do you need?"

"Until Sunday. At the earliest. I suspect your plane is grounded anyway."

"*Oh*, no." Wildly, Mandy shook her head. "I'm done working for Benson. That guy thinks he's some kind of fricking *king*. Expects me to ride out a Cat Three hurricane all alone in this godforsaken place! With everybody else evacuating? And all the houses boarded up for the season? He can't *pay* me enough. I told him he was out of his fricking *mind*, so he tried to fire me. But he couldn't," she finished with palpable satisfaction, "because I *quit*."

Dionis gathered her fraying patience. "When did you talk to him, Mandy?"

Again, the groom glanced at her watch. "I sent him a text. About forty-five minutes ago. I'm not sure it went through, because cell coverage is spotty at Northern Light . . ."

Forty-five minutes ago. While Dad and I were on the water, Dionis thought. *Jesus.* "Look. We've got a lot of people to evacuate. Once we've got them all back to Madaket, we'll call Mr. Benson. But we can't do anything about the horses until we have his authorization."

"I'm going with you, *now*, to Madaket."

Dionis threw up her hands. "You'd really leave the palominos all alone out here? Don't you *care* about them?"

"Sure. But they're Benson's problem, not mine," Mandy retorted. "I'm *not responsible*."

"No," Dionis agreed sarcastically. "I can see you're not."

Mandy wrapped her arms protectively across her chest.

"I've got a seat out on a Cape Air flight to Boston this afternoon."

"Yeah, I'm guessing that's canceled."

The groom reached into her tote bag and pulled out a wallet. "Five hundred bucks. For a spot in your boat."

A few raindrops struck Dionis's face, then a few more. She and Jack charged homeowners and guests two hundred dollars apiece, round trip, for transport to Tuckernuck, along with their supplies and luggage.

"Otherwise," Mandy threw in defiantly, "I'll radio the Coast Guard as soon as you leave! An SOS. I'll tell them you *abandoned* me here, alone."

Mandy would be a pain in the ass until they got rid of her. Dionis snatched the wad of cash from the groom's fingers, pulled up her hoodie against the rain, and walked back to her father.

"We're going to have to come back and get those horses safely into their stalls tonight," she told him, "because there's no way we can get them off this island. That woman's poison. She's threatening to report us for abandoning her in an evacuation zone."

"I'll take her," Jack said grimly, "and call Benson as soon as I reach Madaket. Give him a piece of my mind."

"Tell him he's about to lose his prize palominos. Better yet—tell his *wife*. She may actually care."

Her father rubbed his left arm fretfully. "Of all the lame-ass stunts to pull, this is the lamest. *Summer* people. And their privilege—"

"Dad. Are you okay?"

His faded blue eyes drifted over her. He stopped massaging his arm. "Nothing a good drunk through a hurricane can't solve."

Dionis watched until he'd fended the loaded skiff away from the Tuckernuck dock and circled out to sea. Then she jumped back in the truck and turned it toward China Trade. She hoped Brad Kramer was sober enough to break down the stuff in Elsa's darkroom. And that something would go right on this shitstorm day.

Chapter Six

MUCH LATER, WHEN the Coast Guard came asking, Dionis would swear that she saw the distress rocket go up a few minutes after 5:30 that night because she'd pulled her work skiff away from Jackson Point for the last time at 4:53. The rain was falling in earnest then, the wind gusting to forty knots, whipping her hair out of its untidy clip and plastering it to the right side of her head. She should have been winching the skiff onto its trailer with Ryan Radleigh's help and heading back to town by that time. But life abruptly somersaulted in the hours after she left Tuckernuck with Elsa Chamberlain and her scowling, shivering boyfriend.

Brad Kramer was feeling the effects of a vodka binge—"It seemed a waste to just leave it there for the hurricane"—and the bucketing of the skiff across the deepening swells to Madaket seriously challenged his head. He swayed on his bench seat, hands clamped to his temples.

Elsa Chamberlain ignored him. She was enthralled by the impact of storm winds on the sea, and frustrated, Dionis guessed, that she couldn't halt the skiff and all time to photograph them. Di wondered yet again why two such different people as Brad and Elsa were together—but perhaps only they could answer that question, and only for themselves.

She had felt profound relief casting off from Tucker-nuck for what she'd thought was the last passenger run. There would be a final trip back with Jack, of course, so the two of them could shoo Benson's horses into their stalls for the night, but then they could call Tuckernuck a wrap. Dionis was grateful that she would be warm and dry and safe, soon, from the hurricane's gathering fury. But as she throttled down her engine to approach Jackson Point with the China Trade folks some thirty minutes later, worry unexpectedly knifed through her. A white van was pulled up to the dock, its lights flashing. She could just make out Jake Radleigh's baseball cap and jacket. He was leaning against the van's hood.

"Is that a cop car or an ambulance?" Brad asked suddenly, raising his head.

"Fend off, Ry," Di ordered the elder Radleigh boy. She concentrated on bringing the boat into the dock. Once she had cut the engine, Ryan leaped out to secure the mooring ropes.

"Jake!" he called to his brother. "*Jake*, what's going on?"

But Dionis, helping Elsa clamber out of the skiff while Brad shifted the luggage, had already seen the wheeled gurney, partly shielded from view by the ambulance's open rear doors. A pair of work boots were just visible at the gurney's foot. Her father's boots.

"Sorry," she told Brad hurriedly. "That's my dad." She vaulted out of the skiff and ran.

"Just lost my lunch over the side, Di," Jack explained as she peered worriedly at him. "Right after I helped Ted get the last of his luggage out of the boat. I don't know why he called 911. Just a stomach bug! It'll pass."

Jack's lips were blue, and he was sweating profusely. But his hand, when she gripped it, was ice cold.

"You're the daughter?" asked an EMT—a compact woman of about fifty, Dionis guessed, with unnaturally red hair. She seemed to be in charge of the other two medical techs.

"What's wrong with him?" Dionis demanded. "Why are you taking him?"

"Your father's having a heart attack," the woman said. "Got a car in the lot? Follow us."

SHE COULD FEEL her own heart pounding as she sped erratically behind the ambulance, its siren wailing, along the single-lane Madaket Road. *Thank God it's not summer,* Dionis thought. *Bumper to bumper.* The wind buffeted the cab of her truck and she braked abruptly every time the white van ahead slowed before blaring through a stop sign. Six miles or so from Madaket to the outskirts of town, vehicles pulling to the sandy shoulder ahead of them to let them pass, before the knot of traffic—and an agonizing twenty seconds of lost time—at the turnoff for Quaker Road.

Quaker turned into Prospect, the ambulance slowing to what seemed like walking pace in the heavier town traffic. The van's horns blasted in short, imperative snarls, while Dionis pounded on her steering column— what if Jack *died* while these cars took their sweet time getting out of the way? And then, just before Vesper Lane, the white van turned right, diving into the new hospital's broad drive, and raced for the emergency room entrance.

Dionis had enough presence of mind to park in the

adjacent lot and run. She reached Jack's gurney just as he was being wheeled through the hospital's automatic doors.

"You're going to be okay, Dad," she babbled, running alongside him. Then the gurney swiveled down a corridor and burst through a pair of swinging interior doors. Dionis staggered to a halt, trapped on the wrong side.

"You family?" a man in scrubs asked as he approached her from an intake desk.

Dionis nodded. "Am I allowed—?"

"I'll get you back there as soon as I can. Just take a seat for a moment, please." He gestured toward a chair.

You are not, Dionis raged, *going to ask for my insurance card when my father is dying.* But she sat suddenly, as though her legs could no longer support her. And let her backpack slide to the floor.

"I'm Martin," the man said cordially. "I'm an ER nurse. And you are?"

"Dionis Mather. I'm a daughter," Dionis returned, wanting to scream. "My father Jack was just wheeled past you."

"Also Mather?"

"Yes."

"Great. I just need his social security number."

STORM-CLOUD DARKNESS WAS falling now and Dionis's too-light skiff bucked the harbor whitecaps like a kid on a pogo stick. She was out on the gale-force seas alone. The Radleigh boys had not been able to trailer either of the Mathers' boats by themselves, with Jack's truck at the hospital, and had gone home without telling her, as befit their age and competence. But when Dionis returned to Jackson Point she found the skiffs moored up as securely as the kids knew how. It would not be enough to keep the boats from being hurled onshore in a hurricane, their fiberglass hulls crumpled as easily as candy wrappers. But the boys had done their best, under the circumstances.

"You've got to call Benson's assistant," Jack had muttered to Dionis as another ER nurse—Rebecca, this time—connected him to an IV and a heart monitoring machine. His face had turned gray. "I never got a chance. Take my phone, the number's in there. *Those horses*—"

"Mean nothing right now. Stop worrying about them, Dad, and focus on staying calm. Deep breaths," Dionis soothed.

"The man's a legend," Jack attempted. "*Beloved.* By the entire world! He'll screw our asses to the wall if anything happens to Honeybear or Afterglow."

"You know the horses' names?" Dionis asked, nonplussed.

"Everyone knows their names. They've had their own photo spread in *People.*"

"Benson never hired us to save them. This is his fault."

"But I took Mandy off." Jack closed his eyes fatally. "I'm responsible, Di. I'm the reason those horses are alone."

"I'll handle it." Dionis gripped his hand. "Problem solved. Now try to rest."

Jack smiled faintly, drifting off. It was the morphine, Dionis suspected. She let go of his hand.

TEETH CHATTERING, HER stomach sick with fear for her father and the unpredictable seas she had to face, Dionis took the time at Jackson Point to trailer Jack's skiff. She used anchor lines to lash the whole thing down, insurance against the rising wind. Then she cast off her own mooring rope from Jackson Point and turned her bow toward Tuckernuck.

The skiff rocketed crazily skyward in the rising swells, then slapped down hard as though the sea were made of concrete instead of water. Dionis shivered at the throttle. The temperature had dropped sharply. As Eel Point fell to starboard, the wind slammed against her bow and the skiff yawed, fighting her control. Chill rain pummeled her face and shoulders. *A ski hat would've been smart,* Dionis thought, but there had been no time to stop at home as she'd left the hospital and fought her way west through the high school's afternoon traffic.

She strained to see past the teeming downpour and heaving sea. When she was seven years old, Jack had taught her to stand within the circle of his body and feel the course he made for Tuckernuck. The island's eastern and southern shores were girdled by treacherous shoals, visible at low tide but hidden the rest of the day, and nobody knew the underwater terrain, or understood its moods, so completely as Jack Mather. As a child, Dionis had pictured the sandbars as sucking hands, waiting to snatch at their keel. On NOAA's official charts, the shoals were mere blobs, indicated with dotted outlines— their shifting locations a guess, at best.

She was insane, in these conditions, to be out on the water alone.

Jesus Christ, she thought, and it was a prayer, not a curse. *Let Dad be okay.* When she'd last glimpsed Jack, a trio of medical people had been wheeling him into one of the hospital's brand-new operating rooms.

"He needs a stent," the cardiologist had explained hurriedly. "For a blocked coronary artery." Robert O'Hare wasn't *supposed* to be operating on Jack—he was a cardiac surgeon based at Mass Gen in Boston—but he'd flown over to Nantucket the previous day to board up his Siasconset Bluff house against the hurricane. Nantucket Cottage Hospital knew it. Martin, the ER nurse, had placed the call to Robert O'Hare when Jack's ambulance was still on the Madaket Road. The alternative to surgery was a medevac chopper flight to the mainland. And in this weather . . .

"There wasn't time to get your father out, anyway," Rebecca informed Dionis as she walked her to the waiting room. "Dr. O'Hare is a godsend."

"How long will my dad be in surgery?" Dionis managed.

"Two, maybe three hours. Depending on what the doctor finds." Rebecca studied her stricken face, not without compassion. "Why don't you grab a bite to eat? You can't do anything here."

Dionis had nodded and turned away. *Two hours.*

Her call to Todd Benson's assistant had gone straight to voicemail. No one had returned it yet. But Jack was right—if anything happened to Afterglow and Honeybear on their watch, Benson would put the Mathers out of business. Anxiety wouldn't help her father emerge safely from surgery. She had promised him she'd solve the problem: secure the horses and get back to Madaket, before the hurricane made landfall.

Two hours.

She had no other choice.

As TUCKERNUCK'S OUTLINE grew larger on the horizon by the second, Dionis's bare hands were icy and increasingly numb on the skiff's tiller. The rolling sea was empty of human life.

Which is why, she would explain with utter clarity to the Coast Guard later, she was riveted by the flare.

Or rather, the SOLAS rocket parachute.

That was certainly what it was: a self-propelled pyrotechnic meteor, shooting redly one thousand feet into the dusk off her starboard bow, from the opposite side of Tuckernuck—the *north* shore. No sailor with sense ventured close to the north shore; the water was too shallow in most places, riddled with bars and wildly variable depth soundings that made navigating the seabed off the island's southeastern end seem like a simple game of hopscotch.

As Dionis stared, transfixed, the rocket slowly descended, brilliant as a lightning stab, incandescent for the span of forty seconds. She tried to pinpoint the distress signal. The sandy bluff that banked East Pond blocked her view. But a *rocket*? Not just a handheld flare, or one fired from a plastic flare gun? A rocket meant someone had run aground, or was taking on water, or struggling with a sailboat mast the wind had snapped in half. Or drifting uncontrollably into a hurricane with an engine that had died. Or . . . *suffering a heart attack . . .*

Her skiff was pointed right into Tuckernuck Lagoon's narrow channel. Dionis pulled her gaze from the dying arc of the SOLAS flare and cut her engine. The swells were heaving crazily, throwing her off balance as she scrambled toward the bow. She had no cell phone coverage, but she had a VHF radio and the Coast Guard's band for an SOS, Channel 16.

She used them.

Chapter Seven

CAPTAIN BRUCE FARMER of the US Coast Guard lifted the Jayhawk helicopter off the pad at Joint Air Base Cape Cod at eighteen minutes past six o'clock. He'd been stationed in Sandwich for the past year, and had another three years to go until retirement. He was thinking maybe Hawaii would be fun for his final posting, if his wife, Gayle, would agree to pull Emma—their youngest—out of high school. But tonight, a tropical paradise was mere wishful thinking; Bruce was calculating an approaching hurricane's possible wind speeds and how they might keep him from locating a vessel in distress.

Three other officers rounded out Farmer's crew: his lieutenant commander, Jerry Gonzalez, and two petty officers second class: Vince Schiaparelli and Natalie O'Neill.

The watch standers on duty at Coast Guard Station Brant Point, the venerable clutch of buildings perched near Nantucket's oldest lighthouse, had relayed the call roughly twenty minutes earlier. They'd logged an SOS from a vessel via radio, then an independent report of a rocket parachute fired off the northern coastal shoals of Tuckernuck. No visual sighting of the vessel in distress, and no luck raising that vessel again via radio, despite repeated attempts.

The local Coast Guard response boat could not get close to Tuckernuck's northern shore. The risk of grounding was too great. Particularly in *this* weather. But *this* weather made it imperative to respond to an SOS.

Which meant somebody would have to fly over from Sandwich.

Four Coast Guard choppers were based at Air Station Cape Cod, where they had the flexibility to respond to a crisis anywhere in the region's waters. Seventeen minutes after Brant Point relayed the distress signal, Bruce Farmer was in the air. His chopper had maximum air speed of two hundred miles per hour. He'd reach the target area in roughly fifteen minutes.

Sandwich sat on the northwestern edge of the Cape. Farmer guided the Jayhawk east and south toward the narrow belt of the Cape Cod Canal, black and choppy below, and scanned the unbroken line of traffic snaking across the Sagamore Bridge. White headlights formed a perpendicular line the length of Route 6, the Cape's east-west artery, for at least thirty miles, all the way to Orleans, before turning sharply north toward Provincetown and dwindling from sight. The Cape was emptying out before the hurricane hit.

Despite the wind gusts and pelting rain jolting his rotors, Farmer was suddenly glad he was high above it all. Let them run for Providence or Boston. He was fighting forty-knot winds for control of his bird, adrenaline singing in his veins.

The land fell away beneath him as he reached Nantucket Sound, the manta ray outline of Martha's Vineyard already coming up in his windscreen. He pinpointed Oak Bluffs, then slid the chopper east, fighting the wind playing ping-pong with his rotors. The tiny mass of Muskeget

Island, little more than a haul-out for seals tossed between the Vineyard and Tuckernuck, slipped almost unnoticed behind.

And then, there it was beneath them: the moors and dunes of what his wife called the most exclusive ungated community on earth. *Tuckernuck*.

"Sir!" Natalie O'Neill shouted. She was crouched in the open port hatch of the chopper directly behind Farmer, scanning the sea as she'd been trained. Schiaparelli was doing the same thing at starboard. With sustained winds at nearly thirty knots, the waves below were topping fifteen feet. Farmer stared in the direction O'Neill pointed.

A motor yacht, maybe seventy feet in length, possibly a Hatteras, had grounded on the sandbars just off Tuckernuck's north shore. Swells were breaking over the exposed hull and deck. A *very expensive girl*, Farmer thought, even glimpsed from this altitude and with this poor visibility— worth a couple of million bucks at least. Canted at a crazy angle, and possibly taking on water. He could glimpse no one on deck, no one near her. No black outline of a body clinging to the bow or the stern or the cockpit. Nobody struggling through the crashing surf toward the safety of the Tuckernuck beachhead below.

Then again, the light was going. He could be missing something.

He passed a bullhorn to Schiaparelli. "Hail the vessel."

As the chopper hovered and bucked in the wind, the petty officer complied. The crew waited for a response; nothing.

Farmer squinted as he scanned the Tuckernuck beach, searching for signs of life. This would only get harder as the seconds ticked past.

"O'Neill," Farmer shouted. "Ready the hoist and winch. I'm sending you down."

MERRY HAD THROWN together pea soup before bed the previous evening. Storm weather on Nantucket called for her late grandmother Sylvie's kind of comfort. There was no recipe in Merry's head, just years of watching the people she loved best stir a pot full of cubed bacon and vegetables—chopped shallots, or plain old yellow onions if she didn't have them, diced carrots and celery, some garlic—until they caramelized. Sometimes she used salt pork for the base instead, and other times she used pancetta. Whatever happened to be in the fridge. She deglazed the pot with white wine, stirred the split peas into the shimmering mirepoix, added two quarts of chicken broth, some cumin, a thyme branch and a couple of bay leaves.

Everything had simmered for a few hours until it fell apart, while Merry helped Georgiana make up beds for the kids and caught her up on all the island news.

She was relieved to have the soup this Wednesday night, as she fought the wind gusts slapping the back door of the Cliff Road house. Pocock was demanding every last minute of the hours she'd agreed to serve before her wedding. And the usual responsibilities of the Nantucket Police, keeping order and offering help in a community of some fifteen thousand year-rounders, had been distorted out of all proportion by the hurricane's approach. Merry was later getting home than she liked, and bone-tired.

George, bless her, had tossed a salad and pulled cornbread from the oven. With the smoky goodness of the pea soup, that would be dinner. Comfort food, as the rain battered the old Mason house sitting high above Nantucket Harbor and the wind tugged at the railings of the roof walk.

A fire roared in the living room. Hale Whitney, George's husband, was working on his laptop at one end of the long trestle table. Trey was at the table's other end, manfully composing his first high school English essay despite being technically on vacation. His younger brother and sisters were ignoring what work they had until Sunday, a privilege of elementary school.

"Any word from Peter?" George asked as she counted out forks and spoons.

"He texted," Merry replied. "We're not to wait for him. He and Rafe spent all day harvesting cranberries, and he's a cold, wet mess. He said he'd shower and change at the farm and grab some food when he gets here."

"So, there's seven of us." George gathered a clutch of mats and napkins and silverware and somehow still managed to hook a finger around the neck of a bottle of white wine.

"Trey." Hale closed his computer and relieved her of the bottle. "Take it elsewhere, okay? We need the table."

"Too much gaming upstairs," Trey said. His eyes followed his mother as she emerged a second time from the kitchen. "Hurricane lanterns! Can I light them?"

George tossed him a cylinder of extra-long matches. "Be my guest. Dinner's in five."

A sudden clatter overhead jolted them all to silence as the wind fell on the house like a furious banshee, howling and clawing at the windows.

"Dad," Trey said, awed, "*look*. An Adirondack chair just nose-dived onto the front lawn."

"Flew off the roof walk." Merry carried a tureen of

steaming soup to the table. "I totally forgot Peter and I took a pair of them up there last weekend to watch the sunset. Maybe you and Trey could wrestle the other one into the attic, Hale? Before we all sit down?"

"And call the kids," George added. She turned her back to the fire, looking as though she craved the warmth against the fury of rain. "Glad we're inside tonight, and not in the air. Or on the water."

"Me, too," Merry said. Under the overcast sky, daylight was fading, although sunset would not be for another hour or two. Almost nothing was visible of the world beyond the windows except the towering hedge of ancient privet that edged the front lawn. An impregnable green wall, it writhed now as though lashed by a whip.

Trey dashed across her vision, the hood of a red rain slicker pulled over his head, and lifted the rebel Adirondack chair from the wet grass. As she watched, he heaved it around the corner of the house, making for the old detached garage where she'd left her SUV.

Nantucket homes had weathered two centuries of storms by firelight and candleflame, Merry told herself, and the Mason house would weather this one.

They all had ice cream for dessert. "Better than watching it melt," George mused, "once the power goes out."

NATALIE O'NEILL DISENGAGED the carabiner from her hoist line and reached for the flashlight she carried on her belt. Her other hand was gripped firmly on one of the grounded yacht's gunwales. Dropping from the Jayhawk in forty-knot winds had been hairy enough—she'd swung through the air as the winch lowered her harnessed body—but the canted surface of the deck she'd landed on was slippery with rain. If she lost her balance and went into the water, she'd embarrass herself. The captain could have sent Schiaparelli down—he carried an AST rating, or aviation survival technician qualification, which meant he swam in open water to save shipwreck victims. Natalie was rated HS—a health services tech. She was damned if she'd screw up with three guys watching from the helicopter, bucking the wind gusts as it hovered overhead.

She worked her way carefully to the Hatteras's main deck cabin and shined her beam through the companionway, which was angled at forty-five degrees now that the yacht had heeled on its side.

Involuntarily, Natalie gasped.

A woman was huddled against a kitchen island in the middle of the yacht's galley. Natalie's flashlight picked out the woman's face, dead white; her eyes were closed. But her lips moved as the light hit her.

Natalie slid through the canted companionway, careful not to catch her gear on the frame. In seconds she was kneeling at the woman's side, gloves off and fingers searching for a pulse.

It was only when she'd found one, and reached again for the flashlight tucked beneath her armpit, that she glimpsed the second body.

A man, this time, sprawled facedown across one of the cabin portholes as though he'd been trying to force a way out. He was spattered with something dark that might be oil in the flashlight's beam but was probably blood.

There was a pool of it beneath him, spreading across the glass.

Natalie reached for her radio.

Schiaparelli would have to join her, after all.

Chapter Eight

PETER MASON PULLED into the gravel drive that circled the Cliff Road house that night and hesitated an instant before killing the ignition. There was a small garage on the western side of the property, but it was anything but sturdy, and he'd rather risk leaving his Range Rover in the lee of the three-story main house than inside a building that might collapse under hurricane winds.

Peter thrust open the car door and hustled through the lashing rain to the Rover's cargo door, liberating Ney. He eyed the backup generator Rafe had persuaded him to bring; he'd unload it after he'd had something to eat.

Peter closed the tailgate and whistled for his dog, who was lifting a leg against a hydrangea bush. Then he halted, rain trickling down his face and the neck of his jacket. A pair of headlight beams was snaking from the garage he'd decided not to use, illuminating the rain as it fell. The only car parked there was Meredith's police SUV. George and her family had taken a taxi from the airport the day before.

Ney barked and ran toward the headlights. Peter followed him just as the gunmetal gray hood of Merry's car appeared at the corner of the house. She was staring straight ahead, unaware of him, but Ney's flurried greeting must have caught the corner of her eye and she glanced their way. She broke into a smile and rolled down her window.

Ney rose on his hind legs and thrust his tongue at Merry's cheek. Peter nudged the dog aside and kissed her. "Where are you going?"

"To the hospital," she said. "Sorry. I'll try to make it fast."

"Is somebody hurt?" With a stab of worry he thought of her grandfather; Ralph Waldo was getting frailer.

"Gunshot wound. I'm on call, remember?"

He had completely forgotten. The approaching hurricane had put almost everything else out of his mind for the past few days. But she'd been allowed to take time off for her wedding and honeymoon only because she'd agreed to cover emergencies through close-of-business Thursday, another of Bob Pocock's ridiculous demands. Merry's police chief was constantly asking for proof of her dedication, when she'd been working Nantucket law enforcement for years before he had. Pocock was a sore point with Peter Mason. He thought the man was an ass.

"There's soup in the kitchen," she said hurriedly. "I'll try not to be too late."

"Be safe," he countered. "I'll keep the bed warm."

He stepped back. The car window rose. Merry pulled away, wet gravel chunking under her tires.

Peter watched as her taillights passed through the tall hedges at the drive's end and vanished onto Cliff Road. His palm found Ney's soft head. One of these days he'd stop feeling lonely every time she left.

THE SUMMONS TO Nantucket Cottage Hospital had come from Terry Samson, who as master chief boatswain's mate was commander of Coast Guard Station Brant Point. Merry had worked with him before, when boats and crime intersected in a way that demanded her attention. Terry had called the Nantucket Police Department and asked for Merry by name. He'd made it clear he wasn't simply reporting an accident.

He was listening to an ER nurse when Merry walked in. She shook the rain off her jacket and set her large shoulder bag on a waiting room chair. It held her laptop and charger.

"Hey." Terry strode toward her and offered his hand. "Thanks for getting here so fast, Mer."

"What's going on?"

"We got a report of a flare going up off Tuckernuck earlier tonight. One of our Jayhawk crews out of Sandwich located a vessel grounded off Tuck's north shore and dropped personnel to investigate. But instead of a wreck, they found a crime scene."

"*Crime* scene?" Merry repeated.

"Two people bleeding from gunshot wounds. Captain Farmer flew them here."

"And the boat's still out there, of course?"

"For a little while." Terry nodded. "Listen—I hate to keep the chopper crew grounded much longer. With sustained winds of thirty knots and gusts topping fifty right now, these guys need to get home. But I knew you'd want to talk to them first. In person."

"Appreciate it. They're in the waiting room?"

"Drinking coffee and watching the Weather Channel. You want to see the victim first?"

She nodded.

"Suze?" Terry called to the nurse.

The woman glanced up from a clipboard.

"Nantucket Police detective Meredith Folger." Merry didn't shake the woman's hand; her own was damp and cold. "I understand you're treating a gunshot wound?"

"The patient's not conscious," the nurse said briefly. "But you're welcome to see him."

Merry followed her twenty yards down a hall and into a darkened private room with a bank of monitors ranged along one wall. An IV drip was parked near the hospital bed where a man lay in a gown, his skull bandaged and his eyes closed.

"He was shot in the head?" Merry muttered. She moved to the bedside and studied the still form. The victim's chest was bare, with life-support sensors taped to his pectorals. Oxygen tubes were inserted in his nostrils and his head was completely wrapped in gauze. Impossible to judge the color of his eyes, which were closed, or of his hair.

Terry handed her a laminated driver's license issued by the state of New York. "They found this in a wallet lying near him on the floor."

Bradley Minot, Merry read. A few months past thirty-six, a hair over six feet tall. Sullen in his digital photograph, but weren't we all?

"He was lucky," Suzie murmured. "The bullet just tore off a piece of his skull."

"And he *survived?*"

"So far," Suzie replied. "He's in a medically induced coma while we monitor brain swelling. The doc would like to get him medevacked to Boston, but with this hurricane—"

"I'm surprised the Coast Guard didn't take him straight there," Merry said, frowning.

"Too much loss of blood, too little time," the nurse explained. "We were the closest OR. For him as well as the woman."

"Woman?" Merry glanced at her.

"Also in the boat. Also shot. Only unfortunately for her, in the abdomen." Suzie backed quietly out of the room. "She died in midair."

TERRY AND THE chopper crew were sprawled on a group of plastic molded chairs in the waiting room, foam cups of coffee in their hands. The air station folks wore jumpsuits the distinctive color of tomato soup and their helmets were tossed in a pile on a coffee table. Merry drew up a chair and let Terry introduce his colleagues.

"Detective Folger," he told them, "is the best. We've worked together before."

"Thanks," she said, pulling her laptop out of her bag and looking first at Bruce Farmer. "I won't keep you long, Captain. When were you dispatched?"

Terry interrupted apologetically. "Actually, Mer, I've got all that typed up for you already—the watch standers' reports from Brant Point, the time of chopper dispatch from Sandwich, and the search-and-locate team's targeting."

"Great. Then I'll cut to the chase. If you could tell me in your own words what you found?"

"Petty Officer O'Neill dropped first to the vessel," Farmer said. "Natalie?"

Fingers poised above her keyboard, Merry waited for the young woman.

"I winched down from the Jayhawk to a motor yacht grounded on the shoals just off the north shore of

Tuckernuck. It was about eighteen-forty-eight hours," she said firmly. "The vessel is a Hatteras M75 Panacera named *Shytown*, maybe thirty yards offshore, keeled over in three to five feet of water, with swells breaking at twelve to fifteen feet. I found two victims inside, bleeding from gunshot wounds, and radioed the chopper for assistance."

"I sent Petty Officer Schiaparelli down," Farmer said, "and ordered Lieutenant Commander Gonzalez to lower two rescue baskets."

These, Merry knew, were the Coast Guard's standard square steel baskets, designed to be released from a chopper and then hoisted again with a victim inside.

"We succeeded in raising both victims," Farmer concluded, "and triaged them as best we could. Petty Officer O'Neill has HS training."

"Health services," Terry explained.

"The Jayhawk isn't a medevac chopper," Natalie broke in, "meaning, it's not equipped like a full-blown Flight for Life. Given the condition of both victims, I recommended we get them to the closest hospital ASAP. And even that wasn't fast enough."

"I understand the female victim died en route," Merry said.

"She just bled out." Natalie's voice dropped low. "I was applying pressure to the wound, but internally—"

"I'm sorry." Merry stopped typing at the petty officer's obvious distress. "I'm sure you did all you could."

"The woman said something." Natalie glanced at Farmer, as though asking permission. He nodded slightly. "The name *Matt*. I thought she was worried about the male victim, so I told her he was on the chopper and we were getting them both to a hospital. She grabbed my wrist and gasped out, as loud as she could, 'MATT.'"

"Nothing else?"

"That's when she died," O'Neill concluded.

The New York driver's license said the male victim's name was Bradley. Merry considered this briefly. The dying woman must have wanted to communicate something about Matt—a friend, perhaps? A relative or lover?—but had run out of time. "Terry mentioned a wallet one of you found. Where was that, in relation to the victims?"

"I found it on the main deck as I was strapping the male victim into the basket," Schiaparelli said. "It was lying between the sofa and the coffee table. The furniture was bolted down and didn't move, but the yacht had canted at an angle when it grounded and everything loose was thrown around. I figured the wallet fell off the coffee table."

"Was there anything on the woman? A cell phone, maybe?"

O'Neill shook her head. "There may be a purse or something below deck. We couldn't waste time searching the Hatteras—not with them bleeding—"

Or with Category Three winds and crazy storm surge threatening, Merry thought. Once the hurricane struck, the boat, grounded or no, would be tossed off the bar like a toy.

"Anybody find the gun?" she asked.

The chopper crewmates glanced at each other. Farmer lifted his shoulders. "Not in the main deck saloon."

"No sign of one by either body?"

He shook his head. "Nothing obvious. But the light was failing."

"And the boat's power was out?"

"The engines were off when we reached the vessel," Schiaparelli volunteered, "and it's standard procedure not to start them again until you've done a visual check for structural damage. You don't want to ignite a gas fire or explode an inboard engine with a rescue op underway."

Merry nodded; that made sense. "And despite the bolted furniture, there was a good deal of disorder in the cabin, I assume?"

"Yeah—it was a mess," Natalie agreed.

"Depending on when the gun was fired, it could have dropped beneath a piece of furniture or have been caught under a galley locker."

"Or tossed overboard," Terry added.

Easy to assume, Merry thought, *but we have to at least try to confirm it.* "Did your team anchor the yacht, Captain?"

Bruce Farmer shifted slightly in his seat. "O'Neill and Schiaparelli set out two spare anchors we dropped from the chopper. But I wouldn't expect that boat to be there in the morning."

"It's a crime scene," Merry pointed out. "And a woman is dead."

"Looks like a murder-suicide to me." Farmer rose to his feet. "The killer is probably lying right here in a coma."

Merry closed her laptop. "We don't know that. Not until we can investigate the scene. And we don't have much time. Can you give me five minutes to reach my colleagues—and then I'll join you?"

Bruce Farmer stared at her. "You mean, in the Jayhawk?"

"You *are* planning to fly back to Sandwich tonight?"

"Of course, but—" The Coast Guard pilot's glance

strayed to the weather broadcast on the wall-mounted television.

"What's your flight window? In terms of wind?"

"It's a twenty-minute trip back to Sandwich," he told Merry. "The storm's predicted to come ashore around one A.M., near New Bedford."

"Passing right over this island on its way," Terry put in.

Farmer gave a brief nod. "Let's say, at midnight. If you're asking how long I'll risk my crew and my bird, I'd say no later than nine P.M."

"And it's nearly six-forty-five now," Merry said. "Let's do it."

Chapter Nine

THE HORSE BARN at Northern Light was simpler than Dionis had expected: a single story with a high-pitched roof and open beams, four loose boxes, and the groom's empty studio apartment at the rear.

She'd been forced to hoist herself over the closed electronic security gate, its iron slick and cold with rain, leaving Jack's old truck parked outside. The wind buffeted her body—it was rising steadily by the second, she realized—and she hunched her shoulders against it as she trudged up the paved drive. She ignored the sprawling, gray-shingled main house with its deep wraparound porches that commanded the bluff ahead of her. The house was designed to focus its attention on the beach below, falling away to the sea. Dionis was sure the views were phenomenal on a clear day—or even tonight, with the ocean furiously whipped into crashing rollers fifteen feet high. But she didn't have time to case the Benson estate. There'd be an active security system armed and ready to blast if she tried to force her way in through one of the house's windows or doors. She wondered who'd get the security alert—another Benson assistant, in New York? Somebody at the Nantucket Police Department?

Howie's face, its strong features newly revealed by the

haircut, striking and indelible, flashed through her brain. He'd looked at her differently while she talked over her wine glass at Lola's the previous night, studying her as though she were a puzzle he needed to solve. She wished he were with her. She wished he knew where she was.

The horse barn, unlike the house, was supposed to be unlocked. Mandy had deliberately left it that way, she'd told Jack, so that someone could deal with the horses. The building sat near what looked like a garage, east of the house—did Todd Benson keep a car there, or a genera- tor? The barn had a fenced paddock looping behind it, and the palominos—Honeybear the gelding, and Afterglow the mare—were huddled nose to tail under an open-sided shelter at the far end. They lifted their heads as Dionis approached, and Honeybear whickered. Afterglow ignored her, seemingly focused on some inner misery. Did the increasingly strong gusts of wind and atmospheric hijinks make horses as nervy as humans? Dionis wished she knew. But she had never cared for a horse in her life.

Shivering with cold, she fumbled with the main door's latch and was relieved to discover that Mandy had done one thing right. It was, indeed, unlocked.

Inside the barn, all was quiet and smelled intensely of horses and hay. An automatic light system flashed on as Dionis crossed the threshold, and she found herself standing in a corridor a dozen feet wide, with two stalls flanking her on each side. These were built of wood from the floor up to the height of Dionis's waist—but above that, metal bars reached to the ceiling, with a deep slot perfectly shaped to accommodate a horse's neck above each central stall door. The barn was empty.

She had called the number in Jack's cell phone under the listing BENSON while she drove back out the Madaket Road from Cottage Hospital. And Todd Benson's assistant had actually picked up, instead of letting an unknown caller go to voicemail.

"Mr. Benson is aware that Mandy Bernstein has left her position," said a woman, who identified herself solely as Catherine. "He intends to fly over after the storm to assess any damage. In the interim, he requested that I answer what questions you might have."

"Is he prepared to lose his horses?" Dionis asked bluntly.

"His horses?" Catherine's voice was blank, almost affronted.

"Afterglow. Honeybear. Mandy left them loose in the paddock at Northern Light. We're expecting winds of up to a hundred and thirty miles per hour here by midnight. Not to mention major storm surge that could overrun Tuckernuck. The horses can't be left outside."

"Aren't you going to deal with them?"

"No," Dionis retorted. "I'm willing to go back out to Tuck and check on them right now. Make sure they're fed and watered. But I'm not going to ride out a hurricane in a horse barn. I'm not on your boss's payroll."

"I don't know what to say." Catherine's tone was frosty; Dionis had disappointed her. "You're in a position to help. Why wouldn't you?"

"My dad is in the middle of heart surgery. Tell Mr. Benson. Also, he owes me a thousand bucks."

She'd hung up on Catherine's answer.

Across from Dionis now was a wide sliding barn door, open to the paddock. A horse-sized door. She crossed the floor, which was oddly springy underfoot, and hesitated in

the cavernous opening, gazing across the ring. Honeybear
stared back at her, and sawed his head up and down. Even
from a distance, he looked alarmingly huge. Were horses
like dogs? Could she just call their names, and they'd
come?

"Honeybear!" she attempted, cupping her hands
around her mouth. "Afterglow!" If she could just get the
palominos safely in their stalls, make sure they had food
and water and that the barn was secure, she could race
back to the lagoon and cast off for home.

Jack's half-conscious face swam before her eyes. He
must be nearly through surgery by now. *Hold on, Dad,*
she thought.

Honeybear snorted, thrashed his tail, and turned his
rump on Dionis.

Frustration sparked in her brain. She went back into
the barn, hunting visually for something like a leash,
although she knew that wasn't the right term. A rope?
A lead? Hanging beside two of the stalls were lengths of
nylon cord that seemed to fit the bill, with soft terrycloth
things at the end that looked like muzzles.

Halter, she thought. The word came unbidden to her
mind from a far-off children's book. *Misty of Chincoteague,*
maybe, or *Black Beauty.* One halter was aqua, the other
hot pink. "Boy, girl," Dionis muttered out loud. She
slipped them from their hooks and marched out into the
paddock.

The palominos shuffled their hooves nervously as she
approached, Afterglow crowding closer to Honeybear,
but neither of them bolted. In any contest between a
stranger and the storm, Dionis figured, she was bound
to seem less threatening. She clicked her tongue and

crooned wordless sounds as she neared them, slowing her footsteps and holding out the aqua noose, hoping Honeybear would show her how he was supposed to wear it.

And amazingly, he did.

The horse stepped forward and thrust his nose obediently through the opening in the blue terrycloth. The lead dangled by one side. Heaving a deep breath of relief, Dionis immediately led Honeybear toward the barn, and to her joy, Afterglow followed along behind them without a murmur.

Dionis halted the big gelding by the stall where his halter had hung and fumbled with the door. As soon as it swung outward, Honeybear nosed past her and slid accommodatingly inside. Lacking a halter for Afterglow, Dionis pulled open the stall door beside the gelding and prayed the mare would walk into it. After a slight hesitation, Afterglow did.

"This is too easy," Dionis told them, feeling shaky with something between hysteria and laughter. She ran her fingers tentatively down the white blaze on Honeybear's nose, which he'd stretched over the stall door to snuff in her scent. Afterglow, too, was peering with interest over her door. Dionis saw her gorgeous gold hide flinch, then flinch again, as a howling gust of wind pummeled the open-beamed barn roof.

"Afraid of hurricanes, sweetheart?" she murmured. "Me, too."

She had no idea what to do next. Food and water were the obvious needs, but what did horses eat and how did they drink? If she opened the stall door and tried to enter, would they freak out? Rear up and kick her in the head? Push past her with half a ton of determination and make for the coast? And if they did, how would she possibly get them back into the barn?

"Food," Dionis repeated out loud. "Water."

She glanced at her watch: six-thirty. Jack might even be in recovery. Under the heavy ceiling of storm clouds, daylight was almost gone. Any time to navigate the shoals between here and home was slipping away, fast. She couldn't risk feeling her way out of the lagoon through Tuck's treacherous shoals in the dark.

Standing on tiptoe, she peered past Honeybear's neck into the stall's interior. It was roomy enough, and the straw around his hooves looked fairly fresh and nicely deep. Mandy had done that much, at least, before quitting. Dionis noticed a stainless-steel oval basin bolted in the far corner at nose-height; a water dish meant for a horse. As she watched, Honeybear thrust his nose in it—and automatically, water flowed into the basin.

She felt a sense of relief. But what did he eat?

There was a square contraption bolted to the opposite wall, with a wire-mesh front, and it still held a few wisps of what looked like hay. Leftover from breakfast? The palomino was lipping the feeder forlornly. *Not* automatic, then. But now she knew where to put the stuff—she just had to find out where it was stored.

And then summon her courage to enter the stall.

Dionis looked around the barn, deciphering what she could.

The floor that rebounded underfoot was rubber, she realized; it must be easier on the horses' legs. There were gadgets set into the ceiling—in addition to the automatic lights, she detected infrared heat lamps and the nozzle of what appeared to be some sort of mister. She frowned.

Humidity was hardly a problem on Tuckernuck; could it be for fire safety? Insect control? Bridles dangled from pegs in the far wall, and a pair of saddles sat on a shelf nearby. Below this stood some boots: the green rubber kind for working, and shining leather ones for riding, in multiple sizes. And at the far end of the stable area, two doors.

She opened the one on the right, flicked on the lights, and found Mandy's quarters. A galley kitchen, sofa, unmade bed, TV, and beyond that, a bathroom.

Behind the door on the left was an unfinished storage space with a concrete floor, fronted by double sliding barn doors big enough to drive a forklift through. Pyramids of hay bales and straw for bedding were partially torn open, a pitchfork shoved upright into one of them. Set into the floor in one corner was a drain. Dionis looked at the plumbing curiously—a warm-water spray wand, for giving the horses baths.

She grasped the pitchfork and prodded the end of a hay bale with the tines. A square section, several inches thick, peeled off. She carried it speared on the pitchfork back to Honeybear's stall.

Afterglow whinnied excitedly when she scented the fodder, and pawed her bedding.

Dionis took a deep breath. *Don't kill me*, she prayed.

But just as she set down the pitchfork and reached for the stall's latch, the barn door behind her shuddered open.

The wind. If the barn was that flimsy, Dionis thought, they were all in danger. She turned, then stopped short, her back to the stall and her heart pounding.

"Hey," said the man looming in the doorway. "I saw your light. I need help."

Chapter Ten

"I should go with you," Howie insisted.

He and Clarence Strangerfield, who managed the Nantucket Police Department's Crime Scene Investigations, had met Merry at Cottage Hospital within ten minutes of her summons. The three of them were standing, now, in front of a gurney in the Cottage Hospital morgue. Lying on it was the body of a youngish woman, mid-twenties to thirties, Merry guessed—still clothed in a pair of jeans and a green cotton T-shirt. Her eyes were wide open, with the limitless stare of the dead, and her feet were bare. An earring dangled from her left ear, none from the right. She looked healthy, athletic. No needle marks that Merry could quickly detect. Just a small tattoo of a feather on her clavicle. And a vicious wound in her abdomen that had bled out all over the jade green shirt.

"I'm not sure that Jayhawk can take all of us," Merry told Howie. "Besides, there's work here. I need you to fingerprint this corpse."

He swallowed. "Okay."

Merry met his gaze, not without sympathy. "In this weather, we're not going to get the body over to the Cape for autopsy for several days. That's going to delay our investigation. It's possible I'll find the woman's identification when I get to the boat, but as she died by violence, we should start with prints."

"Get a DNA sample, too," Clarence added. "Swab the inside cheek. I'll give you a sterile sample container."

Merry nodded. "I want detailed notes about anything you observe on the body—bruises, scratches—that might tell us why or how she died."

"I'll take some pictures," Howie managed.

"Clarence? Help me roll her over."

The Crime Scene chief, like Merry, was wearing plastic gloves. He slid his hand gently beneath the woman's shoulders and rotated them to the left; Merry peered at the back of the body.

"No exit wound."

Clarence carefully set the body down.

"I'll ask one of the docs to extract the bullet fragments, Seitz," Merry said, "and I'll need you to observe that procedure."

Howie expelled a sigh. "Should we do the same to the guy in the other room?"

"Unfortunately, he's been cleaned up a bit. And they tell me the bullet only clipped his skull—so it's not retrievable. Take his prints, but leave the DNA. We need a search warrant for that, and I can't get one at this hour."

"Okay."

Clarence left them, in search of an evidence kit for Howie from his crime scene van.

"Seitz?" Merry added, as she turned toward the door.

"Yeah?"

"Go home when you're done and charge your phone

before the power goes out. Type up your notes, if you've got battery and time. I'll be in touch."

"Safe flight, Mer," he said.

HOWIE KNEW THAT she was not the best of fliers.

She had always been terrified, in fact, of plummeting from the sky in a spiraling plane. But helicopters—small, maneuverable, *with rotors that could fall off*, were infinitely, unimaginably worse.

"It's not safe," Peter had said when Merry called to tell him where she was.

"It's the Coast Guard, for chrissake," she replied. "They wouldn't go up if it were dangerous."

He snorted. "That's exactly when they *do*."

But he did not attempt to ground her. Peter understood her commitment to her work, particularly when unexplained death was involved. They had fought that battle long ago. Merry won.

"Because of the storm, this trip has to be quick and dirty. I'll be back in an hour," she told him.

"If you're not back in two—I'm coming to find you."

DIONIS COULD FEEL the horse shifting behind the stall door, impatient for the feed lying at her feet. Honeybear's breath ruffled her hair; he thrust his long head over her shoulder and eyed the stranger at the door. Reflexively, her hand came up to smooth his nose. Velvet nostrils flickered under her fingertips. An unexpected comfort, in odd circumstances.

"This place is so dark," the man attempted. He took a step toward her—a wavering, uncertain step. To her shock, she realized he wore no shoes, and his bare feet were filthy. "When I saw the light—"

"The whole island's been evacuated. There's nobody else here." A second after the words left her lips, Dionis thought, *Shit. Why did I tell him that?* In all her months and years of caretaking Tuckernuck, she had never seen this man. He was not a resident. He could not be a guest. She was certain of this because he had a striking face— dark hair, a square jaw, and deep-set blue eyes, what her father called a *Black Irish* face. She would have remembered him.

He was studying her carefully, as though afraid she might scream, his hands slightly lifted to show her he meant no harm. Her mind stopped its frantic darting, but her heart still raced. He'd appeared out of nowhere. She and Jack would have known if a stray person was on the island, from their house-to-house contact the past three days.

"Where did you come from?" she asked.

"The sea."

And then she understood. The brilliant distress rocket shooting a quarter-mile into the sky, the VHF call she'd taken the time to log with the Coast Guard, and had completely forgotten in her effort to deal with the horses—he was off the boat. Northern Light faced the north shore of Tuckernuck. He'd walked up the beach from wherever he'd wrecked and made for the glow of the barn. It couldn't have been easy, barefoot; the terrain was rough and unpredictable in the dusk.

"Are you all alone?" she asked.

"Yeah." He stumbled forward, and grimaced. There

were darker stains on his jeans, Dionis saw, that might be grease—or blood. He'd wrapped a strip of fabric, torn from the bottom of his shirt, around his right hand. The bandage, too, was soaked with seawater, rain, and blood.

"You're hurt." She stepped toward him as he sat down clumsily on the rubber barn floor. "What happened?"

"Accident," he said. "My yacht grounded. I . . . hurt myself . . . getting off."

His clothes were wet through to the skin from struggling up the sand in the torrents of rain and wind, his hair black with rain. When Dionis touched his hand, the skin was cold as ice. Exposure and loss of blood; both were dangerous. His eyes closed in what was clearly a mix of exhaustion and relief. She worried it might also be hypothermia. He wore only a windbreaker over the torn T-shirt.

"Wait," she said, and darted into the groom's apartment.

There was a stack of towels in Mandy's bathroom—one of them fairly clean. Dionis grabbed this, then yanked the comforter from the bed. "You need to get out of those clothes," she told him, dropping the linens by the man's side. "I'll boil water. There's a stove and kettle in the kitchen. We'll clean that wound and you can stay warm in the comforter. I'll turn the radiant heat lamps on."

"The what?" he opened his eyes and met her gaze, his own bewildered.

Dionis walked to the wall and flicked a switch. Overhead, panels recessed in the ceiling flared orange. "No expense spared," she said with a faint smile. "This place'll be warm in a sec."

He removed his soaked jacket, wincing, then attempted to pull his T-shirt clumsily over his shoulders. Dionis went to help, focusing on his bandaged hand instead of his bare chest. When the shirt lay in a sodden wad at his feet, she ran to the studio's kitchen. "Let me know when you're decent," she called. "I'm boiling that water. I'll try to find some tea."

"Find some whiskey," he said, "and you're an angel."

MERRY SAT CROSS-LEGGED in the steel cage of the Coast Guard rescue basket, her hands gripping the sides for dear life, as Petty Officer Schiaparelli winched her down to the canted deck of the Hatteras. The steel cable connected above Merry's head should have reassured her—it was strong enough to bear many times her weight—but for the way it swung vertiginously in the gale-force winds. The beating *thunk* of the rotors and the sheer immensity of the Jayhawk looming over her, reduced her to the status of insect. She waited for God to swat her out of existence. Below, the sea broke over Tuckernuck's shoals and the prow of the grounded yacht. As Merry swooped lower and lower, the approaching swells grew increasingly cavernous, spume flying from their crests in long, white trails. Her stomach heaved.

She had been insane to risk all their lives in pursuit of evidence.

Then the descent halted, suspending her a yard above the boat's main stern deck. The rescue basket swung like a clock pendulum, but there was something other than water beneath her. Her limbs shaking involuntarily, Merry lifted herself out of the steel cage and set foot on the stern cockpit seats. Clutched at a siderail, and then stood as upright as she could.

The basket immediately started skyward. Clarence would be coming down next.

Merry felt a sharp rush of gratitude for the Crime Scene chief—well into his sixties, comfortably solid, totally unathletic—and his unquestioning support of her ludicrous mission. Clarence would be swearing continuously as he was winched out of the Jayhawk's belly, but having come this far, he would never leave her alone. Merry waited just long enough to see him begin to descend, then made her way slowly through the gangway into the main cabin, following her flashlight's beam.

She paused on the cabin's threshold, took off her rain jacket, and drew a Tyvek evidence collection jumpsuit from a sterile bag. It had a hood that went over her hair. Sterile booties and latex gloves followed. By the time she was covered, Clarence was pulling himself on deck.

"Marradith?" he called.

"In here, Clare. I'm dressed and planning to proceed to the site where the male victim was found. You start assessing the female victim site."

Before they'd all left the hospital, Merry had asked Natalie O'Neill and Vince Schiaparelli to attempt a rough sketch, from memory, of the crime scene. She'd had a nurse copy it. One map was in her pocket, the other in Clare's. It was standard procedure in evidence collection to work outward from the body. Her victims were no longer in situ and their locations were tentative at best, but Merry would work what remained of the scene correctly.

She trained her flashlight on the damp paper now. Natalie had seen the woman first, huddled against the galley island; the man was further forward in the boat, perhaps thrown off the lounge seating when the hull listed. He had sprawled across one of the broad port windows. Carefully, she picked her way toward the yacht's bow, her beam slicing through the dark.

A second beam flared into life behind her; Clarence.

As she stepped forward, a massive wave hurtled into the yacht's canted prow. The deck beneath Merry's feet shuddered and lifted.

They didn't have much time.

Chapter Eleven

IN THE COURSE of his law enforcement life, Howie had never felt so disturbed.

He had worked crime scenes with Meredith Folger before—murder scenes, even. He did not faint at the sight of blood, and the idea of a corpse did not make him squeamish. But as he examined the dead woman lying on the Cottage Hospital gurney, he felt a surge of unexpected emotion. He was staring at someone his age. Nameless, in her final solitude. Exposed to strangers. And yet, she had a life—somewhere, unknown to Howie, were people who mattered to her. They were going about their simple routines. Finishing dinner. Laughing over a moment from the day, perhaps. Without knowing that the woman they loved was *dead*.

He understood, suddenly, why Merry got so angry when she investigated murder. She hated the violation and theft—of this woman's simple days, her happiness and relationships, her individual space in the world. And of course, her possible future. Holding a killer responsible was Merry's attempt to apologize for all that destruction. A private crusade, masked by her very public job.

Howie had never really thought of his work in that way. He liked the complexity of investigations; even mundane ones involving drug busts or stolen property or hit-and-runs by drunk drivers. He was good at putting together puzzles. And he loved being able to do his job on Nantucket—a rare community that was at once intimate and world-class. This was the first time he'd felt shaken and moved by what lay before him. Maybe he was growing up.

Or maybe it's because she's roughly Di's age, too, he thought.

He drew a sheet over the woman's head.

Howie was done with his examination. He'd noted the lack of defensive wounds on her arms or hands, the lack of powder burns on her skin—her killer had never been close enough to fight off. He'd taken pictures of her savaged abdomen. He had noticed bruises in the shape of thumbprints on her neck, and photographed these. He suspected, from their yellowish hue, that the bruises were several days old; whether hands had choked her in passion or anger, this was not what had killed her.

He closed his laptop. The finger and palm prints he'd collected were already sealed in evidence bags; so were the bullet fragments a physician's assistant had pulled from the body. There were at least a dozen of these; the round shot into the victim's abdomen had fragmented in its path through her small intestine, liver, rib cage, and thorax. To Howie, the sheer number of fragments suggested a hollow-tipped full metal jacket. But how many grains the round had held, or whether it was 9 mm or .38, he could not have said. The Crime Bureau forensic lab on the mainland would tell them more.

He paused as he pulled the door of the morgue closed behind him, and stood uncertainly in the corridor. Nantucket Cottage Hospital's new hundred-thousand-square-foot complex was barely a year old, and Howie was unfamiliar with the layout. Signs overhead and a map on the wall directed him eventually back to the ER.

"I'd like to see the gunshot wound patient brought in by the Coast Guard this evening," he told the duty nurse. Her name tag read Rebecca.

She glanced up from her computer. "He's been moved to a private room. I can look that up for you."

"Great. But could I talk to the doc who worked on him, first?"

"That would be Dr. Hughes," she said. But she looked dubious. "Patient confidentiality may preclude her telling you much."

Dr. Hughes was a competent woman roughly a decade older than Howie, who'd helped the police department with crime scene investigations before. The previous summer, on call while the medical examiner was off-island, she had responded to a murder.

"The guy was shot," Howie said evenly. "Could have been an accident, could have been intentional. Either way, police are involved. Right now, I just want to know if he's going to live."

The nurse sighed. "Follow me. We have a family conference room for this sort of thing."

"I WISH LIKE hell we could have gotten that patient medevacked to Boston," Summer Hughes told Howie, "but I just thought it was too dangerous to risk sending a Flight for Life crew out with a hurricane coming. Now, it'll be at least thirty-six hours before we can transport him."

There were no windows in the conference room, no way to assess the state of the storm right now, but Howie thought of Meredith and the Coast Guard helicopter. Summer's caution about summoning a medevac chopper underlined the risks Clarence and Merry were running. The Coast Guard Jayhawk should have been grounded, too. He suspected Meredith hadn't cleared her evidence collection adventure with Bob Pocock. Clarence certainly hadn't; he avoided dealing with the chief whenever possible.

"Is this guy likely to survive thirty-six hours?" he asked Summer.

She blew out a deep breath. "If he does, he'll probably recover entirely. It's the first two days that are critical, with a gunshot wound to the head."

"You know there was a second victim, who died."

Summer nodded.

"I studied the wound to her abdomen—with the help of one of your PAs," Howie said. "The bullet ricocheted through her vital organs. Came out in fragments. That suggests a particular type of round—"

"One that does maximum damage," Summer supplied.

"Yes. Which leads me to ask you: how'd *this* guy survive a headshot?"

The doctor lifted her brows. "Some do. Maybe five percent of all victims. It depends on the bullet's trajectory. I triaged this patient in the ER before Dr. Mendelsohn rushed him into surgery to remove bone fragments and a piece of his skull. There is a trench several millimeters deep furrowed through his cranium about an inch above his ear. He lost some bone and dura mater—that's the outermost layer of the meninges, the membrane that encases the brain—but the shot didn't penetrate to the brain itself."

"So, he was lucky."

She shrugged. "I don't have to tell you that the worst part of any bullet wound is the shock wave that follows a projectile's path."

Howie nodded. It was part of his training to know how to fire a gun—and exactly how a bullet destroyed people. Which was called *wound ballistics*. As it penetrates the body, even a low-velocity round causes a temporary pressure wave that moves outward perpendicularly to the bullet's path. The wave shoves tissue aside—creating a brief cavity, thirty times larger than the projectile itself. Trauma from the cavity's creation and collapse causes hemorrhages. In the brain, that kind of shock wave has nowhere to go—because the brain is contained and bounded by its skull. Traumatized brain tissue immediately begins to swell.

"If the procedure Mendelsohn performed on the victim's cranium works correctly, his brain trauma and swelling should gradually subside over the next few days," Summer concluded. "If that's happening, we should see some evidence of it in the next few hours."

"Did you or your colleague find any bullet fragments mixed in with the bone?"

"No."

"Then I'm confused." Howie rubbed fretfully at his brow. "The female victim was littered with shrapnel. That suggests a hollow-tipped, full-metal-jacket handgun round. If a round like that hits bone—like someone's skull—it should also fragment. This bullet didn't."

"Is that important?" Summer asked.

"Oh, yeah," Howie replied. "It means we're dealing with two different types of rounds. Fired from two different guns."

"So, there were two shooters?" Summer asked. "I suppose that's not really surprising. The victims must have shot each other."

If only it were that simple, Howie thought. "I think it's surprising as hell. Since when do pleasure-boaters pack personal weapons on vacation?"

"I FOUND SOME vodka," she told the stranger sitting on the barn floor. "I'm Dionis, by the way."

"Dionis?" he repeated. "As in, the Greek god of wine?"

"No," she replied, disconcerted. "As in, the beach near Madaket. You know . . . Eel Point?"

"I don't, actually."

She handed him the vodka. "So, you're not from Nantucket."

"I am not."

He had wrapped a towel around his waist while she rummaged in the studio's galley kitchen, and the comforter was draped over his shoulders. He uncapped the alcohol and took a swig, sighing deeply. His eyelids, thickly lashed, creased closed in relief.

"I thought maybe you'd come out of the harbor . . . or were trying to get back . . . when you grounded your boat."

"Are there any paper towels in the kitchen?" His voice, she realized, was weakening. "Any first aid supplies?"

"I'll check."

As Dionis turned back through the doorway, the tea kettle whistle blew. She lifted it off the burner hurriedly and set it to one side. Grabbed a roll of paper towel from the kitchen counter. First aid stuff was probably in Mandy's bathroom. She ducked into it, her gaze drifting to the window.

Shit. It was dark out. Agitation whirled upward through her chest. She couldn't leave Tuckernuck now. And her dad—

Her dad could be dead.

Hurriedly, Dionis pulled open the cabinet beneath the bathroom sink. Three rolls of toilet paper. A plunger. A bottle of toilet bowl cleaner. And at the back, wedged behind the pipes—a small plastic first aid kit with a red cross symbol stamped on it.

She dashed back, prying open the kit as she went. "I don't think it's ever been used."

She handed him the roll of paper towel and stopped short. He had removed the filthy fabric wrapped around his right hand. The wound he exposed was a black-edged hole in the center of his palm. As though someone had set the muzzle of a gun against it and fired.

Which was exactly, Dionis realized, what someone *had* done.

"What happened?" she croaked, the words fighting their way from her constricted throat.

"I told you. *An accident.* I grabbed my handgun as I was leaving the yacht. It went off by mistake."

Why do you have a gun? she nearly asked; but the words died on her lips. Some people liked guns. Felt safer carrying them. She knelt beside him. "How can I help?"

"I need to disinfect this." The blue eyes met hers. "But I need to clean and irrigate it first."

"That's going to hurt like hell."

His lips flickered grimly. "Already does. That water you boiled. Is it still hot?"

"Won't that just burn your hand?"

"Let it sit for a few minutes. It's safe at a hundred twenty degrees."

"How am I supposed to know?" Apprehension rose in her throat; how was she supposed to know *anything* about this complete stranger who'd appeared out of nowhere with a vicious wound from a gun?

"Use some of the water to make tea. When it has cooled off enough to drink, we can pour it over my hand."

"Are you a doctor?" Dionis asked. It would make sense; she knew doctors, Summer People, who owned yachts. And he'd used that word—*yacht.*

"More of an Eagle Scout," he said.

For some reason, the phrase reassured her. Dionis went back to the kitchen for the kettle. Rummaged in Mandy's cupboard until she found some teabags. Poured a cup from the kettle, which was no longer steaming, she noticed. She removed the kettle lid to speed the cooling process and found a mixing bowl stored with Mandy's pots. She took a sip of tea. Still too hot. She thought for a moment, then went for a clean washcloth. She'd glimpsed a pile of them in the bathroom, as though Mandy never used one twice.

High maintenance.

The tea was cool enough, now; she would assume the water in the kettle was, too. Dionis gathered her supplies, then halted in the doorway, feeling like an executioner.

"Let me pour the water, okay?"

He nodded.

"Do you want something to hold, or bite down on, or . . . ?"

"Just do it."

Dionis set the bowl beside him, grasped the wrist of his wounded hand, and held it over her makeshift catch-basin. "One. Two. *Three—*"

He let out a deep gasp, then a string of expletives as the hot water cascaded over and through the bullet wound in his hand.

Dionis counted. Deliberately.

From one to thirty.

The water in the basin turned smoky orange, then red, then a deep maroon.

The wrist she grasped, as firmly as she knew how, shook uncontrollably in her fingers. But he did not fight her.

The water was gone.

She scrabbled in the first-aid kit for a bottle of iodine. And with a deep breath, began to trickle it into the wound.

AS HE PULLED on his uniform jacket, Howie stopped to thank the ER intake nurse before leaving Cottage Hospital. But Rebecca was no longer behind her desk.

" . . . can't think where the woman has got to," Howie heard her say behind an office partition.

"Hello?" he called. "Is anyone available?"

Rebecca, her expression exasperated, emerged. "Officer. Is there something I can do for you?"

"Yes, actually. If someone could contact either me or Detective Meredith Folger regarding the male victim's medical status, if or when it changes, we'd be grateful. I know that when a new shift comes on, that request could get lost—so if you could put it in both his digital and paper file, I'd appreciate it."

"Of course," the nurse said. "I'll make a note of it. With the day we're having, I'd forget my own name if I didn't write it down."

Howie glanced through the ER windows at the torrential rain, falling in slanted sheets, pounding the parking lot. "Is your relief shift bailing because of the hurricane?"

"Wouldn't be surprised." Rebecca's lips compressed. "It's only going to get worse. We have two people on life-support systems right now, and if the power goes out, we'll be spread thin. We have generators, of course, but . . . our ORs have been full all day. The old hospital had *one* operating room. If an emergency C-section shows up, like it did this afternoon, we bump everyone else out of the surgery line who wasn't critical. *That* wouldn't have worked a few hours ago. We had the gunshot wound, a C-section, *and* a heart attack with coronary stent today. All within hours of each other."

She stopped, exhausted.

"Wow," Howie murmured, impressed. "I hope you get to go home soon. You've earned a night off."

"That reminds me—another note I've got to write down." Her blonde brows drew together, frowning. "This woman hasn't come back. I told her to go get some dinner while her dad was in the OR, but she's never returned."

"Want me to put out an APB?" Howie joked.

Rebecca's expression was troubled. "I might. It's weird—she was a wreck when her dad was brought in. Terrified he was going to die. He had a heart attack out at Jackson Point, right on the boat landing. And then— *poof*. He goes into surgery, she disappears! Nearly four hours later, and there's no sign of her."

Jackson Point. *The boat landing.* Father and daughter.

Howie stared at the nurse, his chest tightening. "You don't mean Jack Mather? *Jack* had a heart attack?"

"You know him?"

"It's a small island. I'm a cop."

The nurse folded her arms over her chest. "I mean—patient confidentiality . . . I shouldn't have . . ."

"You're telling me *Dionis Mather* hasn't come back to check on her father?"

"I called her cell when her dad reached recovery," Rebecca said. "She never picked up."

Howie felt a chill settle over his heart. "Thanks for letting me know."

Chapter Twelve

MEREDITH FOUND THE Glock a few seconds before she was about to give up her search and abandon the grounded yacht completely.

It was a 9 mm G17 Gen5 centerfire pistol, quite new, she suspected. It was wedged between the built-in wrap-around sofa's cushions, almost as though Bradley Minot, the man who'd been found lying on the nearby window, bleeding from a gunshot to his skull, had shoved it under his seat before losing consciousness.

It made no sense.

Merry balanced herself as best she could on the canted and rolling main deck, staring down at the pistol. If Bradley Minot had shot his female companion, then himself, the gun should have fallen out of his hand. And if the reverse were true—if the *woman* had fired at him first, then turned the gun on her own abdomen—the Glock should have been lying near the kitchen island for Clarence to find.

Carefully, she fixed her flashlight beam to illuminate the weapon's position and snapped a photograph of it. Then she secured the weapon in an evidence bag. There ought to be prints. She hoped they weren't smeared.

Merry photographed, as best she could, the pattern of

gouts of blood on the window and sofa cushions. She'd already collected blood and fiber samples from the site for analytic comparison. Finally, she took a close-up of the window's tempered glass. It was crazed with a spiderweb of lines radiating from a single round hole.

The bullet that had trenched Bradley Minot's skull had penetrated the glass and was lost in the churning sea.

"Clare!" she shouted, above the tearing wind.

"Down below, Marradith!"

She groped her way through the cabin in the direction of his voice, her flashlight picking out oddly detached details—visual vignettes—of a truly spectacular boat in utter disarray.

Merry had never been aboard a vessel like it, her own experience tending to fishing or sail boats. This was the sort of craft that docked in the Nantucket boat basin during the summer months, floating luxury that recalled a Manhattan penthouse. The walls were lined with padded ivory leather and some dark wood she thought might be wenge. The galley counters were thick white marble. When she danced her beam forward to the bow, she discovered the dining banquette, two glass and metal tables bolted to the deck among comfortable leather cushions for eight. The staircases leading above and below—she couldn't call them gangways, because they were truly flights of teak steps—were encased in paneled glass with chrome railings.

Clarence's voice had come from one of these.

She had to crawl her way sideways down the stairs because of the angle of the listing boat. The sense of claustrophobia was greater when she emerged into the lower deck's passage, cocked sideways like the one above.

Where the main deck was a great room, this was a narrow hallway. The shifting of the hull was amplified down here, but the noise was muffled. Merry felt her visceral awareness of danger spike. If the yacht were blown suddenly off the bar—if it began to drift in the gale-force winds—

"Where are you?" she called out.

"Aft cabin."

It was immediately to her right, at the foot of the stairs, but the doorway was tilted at a forty-five-degree angle. Trying not to think of the final scenes from *Titanic*, she shone her flashlight through the opening and caught Clarence's backside. He was bent over one of the built-in wardrobe doors, examining the contents under his own light. Merry's beam wavered around the room; it had the elegance and comfort of a hotel suite. Bedside tables and lamps, bolted down. Luxury linens, scattered now from the king-sized bed. A wall-mounted flat-screen TV. She leaned in and discovered the doorway to an adjoining bath. Nicer, from what she could see, than her own at home.

"I've found a weapon," she told Clarence. "Nine-millimeter Glock."

"I found a purse tucked up against the galley cabinets," he replied, "where it probably slid when the boat heeled."

The yacht shuddered violently, and Clarence lifted his head, listening.

"We should get off," Merry said urgently.

"Ayeh," he agreed. "Just pass me a plastic evidence bag, will you? I'm all out."

Merry drew one from the belt around her waist. "What're you looking for in the drawer?"

He held up something the size of a brick, wrapped in plastic. "One of these. Found a dozen or so in the forward cabin."

Merry stared, a wave of heat rising upwards from her stomach. Clarence's brick was the color of curry powder, sealed in transparent plastic and gray duct tape. "Is that . . ."

"Raw, uncut, heroin," he finished.

"WHAT'S YOUR NAME?" Dionis asked bluntly as she finished tying gauze around the bandage she'd packed in the stranger's wounded hand.

"Joe." Feebly, he tried to flex his fingers, and hissed sharply with pain.

"I'm going to fix you a sling so you can immobilize that arm as much as possible—it'll hurt less that way."

"Thank you," he said, "Dionis."

She found a spare sheet and cut it into strips with scissors from the kitchen utility drawer. One length tied Joe's forearm to his neck; another swaddled his upper arm tightly to his ribs. He grunted as she pulled the strips tight, but looked relieved when his hand no longer dangled freely.

"Would it help you to lie down? There's a bed in the other room."

Joe nodded. "I'm feeling really lightheaded."

"I'm not surprised. You must have lost some blood." She rose to her feet and grasped his good shoulder to steady him as he pushed himself upright. He wavered, and she clutched him around the waist, or what she could find of it through the swaddling comforter. "Can you make it?"

He threw his left arm over her shoulders and she

helped him walk slowly into the groom's quarters. When he sank down on the bed, he sighed with relief.

"I'll see if I can find us some food in a bit," Dionis told him, "but first I've absolutely got to feed these horses, or they'll kick their stalls down."

"I'll be okay," Joe assured her. His eyes were already closed. He braced himself with his good hand and swung his legs onto the mattress. "No rush."

Honeybear, who had seemed placid enough when Dionis had entered the barn half an hour ago, was turning restlessly in his box. Afterglow was pawing a ditch in her straw bedding and snorting repeatedly. Dionis wondered if the smell of blood had affected them, or if the horses were simply agitated by the weather system battering the barn.

The adrenaline rush of Joe's unexpected appearance and all he'd required her to do had dispelled Dionis's fear of the animals' size. She was grimly preoccupied with the job at hand, and knew that more difficult ones awaited her beyond the barn door. She lifted the block of hay off the pitchfork she'd abandoned on the floor and unlatched Honeybear's stall door.

"Hey, sweetheart," she crooned, holding out a large handful of fodder beneath the horse's nose. He snatched it and calmed immediately, rhythmically chewing. Dionis edged past him, pulling the door closed behind her. The feeding rack was to her left. The door at its top opened easily and she stuffed the hay inside the metal bars, packing it tightly. Honeybear nudged her shoulder. She stepped back, allowing him to reach his feed, and sidled sideways through the stall door again.

She took a deep, shuddering breath. *Piece of cake.*

She fetched a second block of hay with the pitchfork and repeated her maneuvers in Afterglow's stall. The mare was showing the whites of her eyes, nervy as hell, but when Dionis offered her a handful of hay she lipped it, snorting effusively. Dionis hoped the food would settle her down.

She dusted off her hands once she was safely on the far side of Afterglow's door. If she ever got home to her laptop, she was going to research horses. Being able to handle them seemed like a life skill she ought to have.

The sound of purposeful chewing reminded her that she had not eaten since breakfast—not since . . . *Dad*.

The thought of Jack cut through Dionis like a knife. She ran to her backpack and pulled out her cell phone. With all Todd Benson's money, surely, he must have cell coverage at Northern Light?

Dionis watched her network search, and search again. No service.

She glanced through the barn windows. Darkness had completely fallen. Impossible to navigate the sea between Tuckernuck and Madaket, now. Impossible to get to her father's bedside at Nantucket Cottage Hospital and know for herself whether he was going to survive or leave her. He would think she'd abandoned him. Or he'd remember she'd gone to Tuckernuck—and be terrified her boat had capsized in the storm.

Her boat.

The work skiff was her last link to home. The way she'd left it, moored to the floating dock, the boat would never ride out a hurricane. The dock itself could be trashed by morning. She absolutely had to pick up one of the moorings in the lagoon, in the hope it would anchor her skiff through the storm. Otherwise, she'd be stranded here, and with no way to let anyone know where she was—

Panic leapt in her throat.

That quickly, Dionis decided. She would walk out to her parked truck and drive toward the lagoon. It might be her last opportunity tonight. If she was lucky, she'd run into a random spot of cell coverage on the way and call Cottage Hospital. If not, she could at least secure the skiff.

She leaned through the studio apartment doorway. "Joe?"

No reply except even breathing.

She rubbed Honeybear's nose, slung her backpack over her shoulder, and braced herself to enter the wind.

Chapter Thirteen

HEADED FOR JACKSON Point, Howie slowed his car to a crawl as he crossed the western end of Hither Creek. Ames Avenue was awash in a rain and wind-fueled storm surge, lapping at the tops of his tire wells. The Atlantic Ocean was driving straight across Madaket Beach, swamping the road, and spilling into the creek on the far side—which, like so many bodies of water on Nantucket bearing the name "creek," was in fact a marshy inlet of a bigger harbor. In this case, Madaket Harbor.

He'd taken a few minutes to look in on Jack Mather before he left Nantucket Cottage Hospital. He was being transferred from Recovery to a private room at that very moment. Howie had met up with Jack there. Dionis's father was still slightly groggy but coherent. He'd grasped Howie's hand.

"Where's my girl?" he rasped.

"That's what I wanted to ask you," Howie had replied. "The doc can't reach her to give her your update."

"She must still be on Tuck." Jack closed his eyes. A nurse was settling him into bed, raising the top to sitting position so he'd be comfortable, arranging the feeds of his IV. "She went back one last time while I was in surgery. For the horses."

"Horses?"

"Todd Benson's. He never got them evacuated before the storm."

"Oh, Christ." Howie knew all about Todd Benson—the man was an icon in New England—and his spread out on Tuckernuck. "When did Di leave?"

Jack grimaced fretfully. "That's just the thing, Howie! *I don't know*. I was pretty far out on morphine at the time. Two hours ago? Four hours ago?"

Four hours, Rebecca the nurse had said. Howie squeezed Jack's hand, tamping down on a sudden flood of anxiety. Dionis had gone back out on the water. With a Cat Three descending on her head. "Don't worry, sir. I'll track her down. Make sure she's safe. I'll bring her back to see you, okay?"

"Okay." Jack sighed. "Tell her I love her, will you?"

Now, Howie peered through his rain-lashed windows into the darkness. On the left, the beach had vanished. On the right, the tips of Hither Creek's marsh grasses could barely be glimpsed in the swirl of inundating sea.

He pushed on carefully, not wanting to find himself cut off from the road back to town. The bridge flood diminished somewhat as he progressed further up Ames Avenue and left Hither Creek behind. Then he turned right and made for Jackson Point, stopping short well before the boat dock.

Once again, the road ahead was inundated. This time, from Madaket Harbor itself.

Howie pulled into the Jackson Point parking lot and killed his engine. He pulled his rain jacket hood over his head and, pushing hard against the wind, forced open his car door.

Goaded by the storm, it slammed immediately behind him. Between the rain and the darkness, Howie could barely see. But he knew enough to circle the parking lot first.

There were three trucks still sitting there, and one boat on a trailer. Howie recognized Jack's Dodge Ram, which Dionis would have driven from the hospital to Jackson Point, and Jack's work skiff. She must have trailered it and left it securely here before casting off from Jackson Point on her last run to Tuck. She'd cleated mooring painters to the boat and buried their anchors in the parking lot's sandy loam to secure them.

He trudged out of the lot and through the swirling groundwater toward the boat landing.

Seawater broke over his ankles, then his calves, and finally reached his knees. The dock was lost beneath encroaching Madaket Harbor, which hurled waves over the bench where boaters and tourists usually sat.

Dionis's work skiff, as he expected, was nowhere in sight.

Howie stared out toward Eel Point, the harbor's distant arm, just discernible from a scattering of lights. Those would be from the windows of permanent residents who hadn't evacuated, riding out the storm. But to the northwest, in the direction of Tuckernuck, nothing was visible.

He was not religious in the slightest. But he hoped and prayed tonight that Dionis had berthed her skiff somewhere snug and stayed with Todd Benson's horses. If she'd tried to reach home, and never made it—

"Be safe, Di," Howie whispered into the wind. "*Please.*" Sick at heart, he turned away from Jackson Point and fought his way back to his car.

SHE WAS THINKING of him at almost the same moment, far across the water on Tuckernuck, in her father's battered old truck pulled up on the bluff.

Dionis stared through the squalling night toward a few faint sparks—red, white, green—that wavered, disappeared, and reappeared. *Madaket.* The truck rocked in the wind. She did not want to open the door and force her way out. But she must.

She steadied herself against the gale, head down, and made her way to the edge of the bluff. Everything about the night was unstable, unpredictable, deadly. The sea was washing over the floating steel gantry moored to the dock. She could pick out the pale gray hull of her work skiff through the turbulent darkness. It bucketed crazily along with the dock, which was pitching in the storm surge like a paper cup in a rain gutter. The narrow sickle of beach that rimmed Tuckernuck's Lagoon was completely underwater. So were the two dinghies her father kept overturned above the usual high tide line.

Gone. The dinghies were gone.

Dionis had intended to row one of them to her skiff, tie the dinghy behind it, then cast off from the dock and steer the skiff out to the nearest mooring buoy. The buoys marked the most secure place to moor in Tuckernuck's lagoon, because they were attached by heavy galvanized chains to pyramid bottom anchors, buried up to their necks in the seabed. Dionis and Jack had placed the anchors, strong enough to hold Jack's fully loaded barge, themselves. It took a lot to move embedded iron. Picking up a mooring by herself in gale-force winds would be a bitch to manage, but it was her last hope of saving her boat once the hurricane hit.

Without a dinghy, however, the process was exponentially harder. Without a dinghy, she would have to swim from the moored skiff back to shore.

Dionis returned to the truck, removed her sneakers, socks, sweatshirt and jeans. The air temperature was chilly, but the sea would be colder. Nantucket Sound averaged sixty degrees in September, but tonight, under storm conditions, Dionis thought it would be closer to fifty-five. *Bracing.*

Her skin rippled with gooseflesh as soon as she stepped back onto the sand that led down to the dock. The wind nearly lifted her off her feet, and she bent double to increase her center of gravity, fighting back against the gale. The floating dock was like a funhouse floor, bucking and dipping at a crazed angle, slick and cold underfoot with rain. Dionis grasped the handrails, her teeth gritted, and felt the storm plaster her hair to her head.

She was shaking with cold and adrenaline by the time she stepped into the skiff, and the boat was roiling so much in the fierce waves that she slapped her left leg hard against one of the seats and sprawled facedown in the bilge. Spume broke over the bow and drenched her from head to foot. She yelled ferociously into the wind to summon her nerve. Then she hunted deep in a forward locker for a spare jacket to throw over herself while she worked. Her shaking intensified. Her bare legs felt like they were on fire. She untied the painter that held the skiff to the dock and fell back toward the stern. Then, one hand on her outboard engine, Dionis paused for an instant to draw breath. She fended off from the deck, grasped the engine starter, and yanked it.

On the fourth try, the skiff heaving vertically in the waves, the engine caught.

She was tempted—*so tempted*—to fight her way back to Nantucket despite the darkness. Tuckernuck's girdle of shoals would be irrelevant in the storm surge she was witnessing, lost far below the keel of her skiff on this insanely high tide. But these waves in the relative protection of Tuckernuck's Lagoon were dauntingly steep. The skiff was absurdly light. Out in the more open water between here and Madaket, the sea could swamp her.

And there was Joe to consider. She was wary enough of his wound and his story to leave him there safely snoozing in Mandy's apartment, and cut for home; but was that unethical of her? Was it *fair*? Once the Coast Guard arrived, after the storm had passed, to examine Joe's stranded yacht, he'd have quite a tale to tell of her abandonment in an emergency. And there was probably nothing weird or wrong about his story or his wound *anyway*. Just an accident, as he'd said—

Resolutely, Dionis turned toward the direction of the mooring buoys, only a few dozen yards away. They were large red spheres quite visible in daylight but far more difficult to discern now, bobbing on the tortured sea at night. She felt her way, squinting as though that might help. Saw the first one come up in her running lights only when it was about to slip past her—but on second thought, it was farther from shore than she liked. There was another buoy between this one and the sand. She turned to starboard and cut the engine. As the wind and current pushed her shoreward, Dionis ran to the skiff's bow, mooring hook in hand.

Her heart in her throat, she leaned over the pitching gunwale, trying to gauge the surge and the buoy that seemed to be rocketing toward her suddenly. She slid the hook into the water, hoping against hope she'd catch the mooring's pickup line—and grazed the top of the buoy.

Twice more, Dionis fired the engine, came around, and tried for the buoy. The waves were getting higher and more violent with every passing second, and the wind was shifting—so that it grew harder to calculate her drift and speed. Her teeth were chattering now and her hand shaking so badly she could barely keep a grasp on the mooring hook. This time when she ran from engine to bow, she threw herself flat on the skiff's gunwale, her feet locked beneath its seat. If the hook caught the mooring pennant and jerked her arm as the skiff floated past, she did not want to be pulled overboard.

It was difficult to see the pennant in the pitch black, even with her running lights, but she made a desperate scooping motion with the hook this third time and came up with a pale gray pickup line that gleamed faintly in the darkness. Sobbing, Dionis clutched at it with her other hand. Her fingers were insensate with cold, slick with rain, and the line was coated in seaweed. It nearly slithered snakelike away from her. Dropping the boat hook into the body of the skiff, she held on grimly to the cold, wet, slippery mooring pennant with all ten fingers furled like claws. Then she hauled, hand over hand. The mooring came up suddenly against the skiff's bow. Dionis fumbled for her painter. She took a maddening number of seconds to run the painter through the pennant and secure it back to her cleats.

This done, finally, she lay prone for an instant, her shaking fingers draped over the skiff's gunwales.

Then she forced herself up and reached again into her forward locker. Drew out a second painter. This one she ran through the steel eyelet on top of the buoy itself and knotted it repeatedly to the skiff's port cleat. The boat would turn, now, on the mooring to face into wind and tide, taking the storm's force at the point of least stress— the bow.

It was the best Dionis could do.

She shoved everything loose that remained in the skiff inside the lockers, hoping to save what she could from the sea's wash. She raised her engine and zipped on its cover. Then she rested for another moment, hating the necessity of removing her jacket. But she could not afford the extra weight. She pulled it off and felt it torn instantly away from her—lifted on a gale of wind to swirl out over the sea. Her signal flag to the vanished world.

Dionis watched until it merged with the darkness, indistinguishable. She was epically small against the rage all around her. A fruit fly. A minnow. She strapped a life vest she'd taken from the locker around her torso. Then she braced herself, and slipped over the skiff's side into the heart-stoppingly cold water.

Chapter Fourteen

"THANK GOD," PETER said, as Merry blew through the front door at ten minutes past nine that evening. He'd stopped pacing the hall when she called from the airport and he knew she was safely out of the Coast Guard Jayhawk. But that had been more than half an hour ago, and he'd started to worry—about car accidents, downed power lines, flooded roads. Trees falling over just as Merry drove beneath them.

"Clarence and I had to drop a load of evidence at the station," she explained. "God, I have never been so tired in all my life."

"Tea? Warm milk?"

"Bourbon," she decided. "In a big-girl glass. I've been cold and damp for hours, and I'm sure some nineteenth-century doctor would assure me whiskey's medicinal."

"Go change," Peter advised, "then come back down by the fire and tell me all about it."

"Where are the Whitneys?" She glanced in surprise around the quiet house.

"I sent them to the Dreamland. Could be the last time it's not flooded this weekend."

"True." The Dreamland was Nantucket's only real movie house, although fusspots on the southern end of the island argued that movies were *also* shown during the summer at the 'Sconset Casino. The shingled building sat on Water Street, one block off the steamboat wharves, which meant its ground floor was occasionally damp during storm season. It would definitely be closed tomorrow. Everything on Water Street would be closed.

She dropped her bag in the hall, her soaked shoes and coat in the kitchen, and took the back staircase up to the master suite where she and Peter were staying. The wind was shrieking around the old house, and the double-hung casement windows—original, with the rounded inset mark of Colonial glass—rattled in their frames. They hadn't had the time to board up most of them, and Merry felt a finger of worry tease her spine. Hurricane-proofing Mason Farms had taken priority. But Isaiah Mason's 1820 frame house on the Cliff had withstood terrible storms before, she reasoned; surely it would do so again?

Hot water streaming over her hair and down her chilled back restored her. So did warm pajamas and fleece slippers.

Peter had set out some cheese along with the bourbon and joined her in a glass.

"It's like an unexpected date night," Merry told him, drawing a throw around them both as they sprawled on the sofa facing the fire.

Peter's lips found her temple. "You smell like a warm infant. With a regrettable distillery habit. Now tell me why you risked your life tonight."

"Evidence," Merry said, "that I was afraid might wash away."

"Of what?"

"Murder."

She told him then about the grounded yacht and the woman who'd died before she could reach the hospital. And about the cache of drugs she and Clarence had hoisted into the belly of the Coast Guard chopper, along with their baskets of crime scene evidence.

"Sixteen *kilos?*" Peter repeated.

"Worth a street value of a couple million. Or so the Coast Guard tells me. Biggest haul in the Cape and Islands District this year. We're going to split the credit with the Jayhawk crew when the story hits the news."

"I think you've earned a day off tomorrow."

"I wish." Merry popped a hunk of cheese in her mouth and chased it with a sip of whiskey. She leaned her head on Peter's shoulder, muscled and solid as a bolster. "Pocock's threatening to rescind my leave if the storm's bad enough."

"Nope," Peter said decisively. "Not happening. We're going to party in the rain this weekend and be on a plane to Paris Monday. If Pocock tries to pull anything, I'll tender your resignation myself."

Merry sighed, her eyelids fluttering. The flames were melding to a blue and orange line beyond her half-closed eyes. "You can't do that, Pete."

"Why not?"

"Because swinging out over the ocean tonight, scared out of my mind in gale-force winds, I realized something important. Something even Bob Butthead Pocock can't ruin."

"What?"

"How lucky I am," she said. "Do you know how *lucky* I am? To love what I do?"

Peter's gaze, warm and probing, met hers. "I know how lucky *I* am." He kissed her.

"TERRY," HOWIE SEITZ felt an instant of relief as the Coast Guard chief picked up at Brant Point Station. "I was afraid you'd have gone off duty."

"Not tonight," he replied. "Not tomorrow either. Just drinking coffee and checking screens."

"You and me both." Howie rocked back in his chair at the police station. He'd driven there straight from Jackson Point, his anxiety mounting, to turn over the fingerprint and bullet fragment evidence he'd collected. He could have done both in the morning, but he was too worried to go home and sit alone in his apartment, waiting for the hurricane to fall howling on his rooftop. He wanted to be *doing* something. Typing up his hospital notes was something.

"Did your chopper get back safely to Air Station Sandwich?"

"Touched down at eight fifty-seven. What's up, Seitz?"

"I'm worried about a friend. I think she's out on the water. Have you received any distress calls from off Madaket tonight?"

"Just the one," Terry replied.

Howie's stomach turned over. "What one?"

"The VHF call we logged at five forty-eight. Woman reported seeing a flare off the north side of Tuckernuck. We got an SOS signal from the yacht, too—that's why we sent out the Jayhawk cowboys. I reported the whole sequence to Meredith via email, but I guess you haven't seen that yet."

"I haven't," Howie admitted. Merry knew nothing about his private life. And she hadn't had time to forward Terry's report. "Who sent you that radio call?"

"You think it might be your friend?" Terry paused an

instant, tapping keys. "Dionis Mather. Isn't she Jack
Mather's girl? The Tuckernuck caretaker?"

"Yeah," Howie said. "And Terry? She's missing."

THE UNDERTOW WAS the first thing she felt, powerful and relentless, as the storm surge gathered, folded, and
cleaved the sea. The shocking cold was an afterthought
to the fierce grip of the waves as they clutched Dionis under
the arms and tossed her forward, like a child thrown off
a swing. She paddled wildly, the life vest keeping her
mouth above the crests that lifted and crashed over her,
flushing the air and sense from her body. Gasping in a
trough, she shook her head, trying to clear her eyes and
brain. Then a wave smacked over her head again. She
was already weak from lack of food, from fighting for the
mooring. Already close to hypothermic from cold. She
was struggling against the current, and losing.

She glanced back and saw the work skiff surge at its
mooring, until another crest blocked out the sight and
she ducked her head beneath the spume. Rising as the
wave passed, she looked around frantically, searching for
the bluff—and realized the tide was coming in. The sea
was driving her shoreward.

Dionis went limp, no longer fighting. Her teeth chat-
tered uncontrollably, but if she allowed the crests to carry
her, buoyed as she was by the vest, in a few seconds her
feet would touch sand. She was lifted and hurled forward,
a wave battering her head, and felt her left leg scrape
hard against something—the galvanized chain of another
mooring. She fought the impulse to grab on to it and rest
for a few seconds. The cold was a greater danger, now,
than the sea; she had to get out of both.

Dionis stumbled, her foot bending double as it dragged along the bottom. She had reached what used to be the beach. She fought to a kneeling position, but another wave broke over her and dragged her back. She reached forward, desperately, and pulled herself further toward shore. The bluff was close, now. But there was no longer a beach where she could haul herself out—

She lifted her head, searching for the faint glimmer in the bluff's darkness that might be the path cut between dune grass, leading up to safety and her truck. If she could find where the path met the water—

Her hands scrabbled among granite stones, whirling in the spray. They cut her skin like knives and tore at her nails. The same tide thrusting her toward shore was simultaneously dragging her west and south, away from the path. She was drifting down toward the lagoon's sandy promontory, known as Whale Island. If she were swept around it, Dionis would be carried out to sea.

Dionis would drown.

She waited for a trough in the oncoming surf and forced herself to rise. To stand. The next wave threw her bodily against the face of the bluff, and she clung to it, spread-eagled and shuddering. The angry sea clutched at her feet and ankles, wanting to drag her back, but she dug her fingers into the wet bluff loam and held on, waiting for the next trough. When it came, she forced herself to inch to the right along the face of the lagoon, clawing her way eastward.

She found the upward path when she fell over it. The narrow trail to the bluff's crest was now underwater to the height of Dionis' knees. Sobbing for breath, she began to crawl upward, bracing her trembling feet against the path's edges and reaching for clumps of dune grass with her chilled, insensible hands.

Halfway, beyond the reach, at last, of the licking waves, Dionis lay still, her face pressed into the earth. The wind howled over her, stinging her cheeks and hair with blown grains of sand. She was shuddering uncontrollably but she could not summon the will to move forward. The cliff seemed impossibly high, the path endless, and her mind urged her to burrow deep and drift away. She clutched her hands beneath her chest and warmed them there. Some-one would come soon. Someone would find her and lift her up, wrapped in a comforter of goose down. So warm, and she was so freezing, her jaws tapping together rhyth-mically. She felt her heartbeat slow and her breathing space to almost normal. She could sleep here. She'd be fine. The bluff would protect her. Why had she thought the storm was deadly? She was a child of the hurricane and the sea.

Clear as day, Howie's voice barked in her ear.

Di. Get the fuck up.

Painfully, she hauled herself the rest of the way up and over the bluff's edge. She crawled on all fours to her truck.

Dionis fumbled in the darkness for her front tire. Clutched it. Then forced herself, shaking, to her feet. Held on to the bracket of her side mirror with one hand, and pulled at the door handle with the other. Her entire body was trembling ferociously now.

The wind thrust back against the truck door. The wind did not want it to open. The wind did not want her to live.

Di, Howie shouted.

Whimpering, Dionis threaded all her fingers into the crack between the truck's door and its jamb, and pulled.

Chapter Fifteen

"MERRY," HOWIE SEITZ asked. "Did you see anybody out there on Tuckernuck when you flew over tonight?"

"You mean, near the boat?" Merry was tucked up in bed with her cell phone, her eyes half focused on the master bedroom's television. Peter was leaning against the foot of the bed, brushing his teeth as he watched the latest weather broadcast. The storm tracker graphic showed a spiraling red blob zeroing in on New Bedford. Nantucket was directly in its path.

"Anywhere on the island at all," Howie persisted. "A truck parked near East Pond or the lagoon, maybe, or a boat moored at the dock?"

"I wasn't looking for that," she said tiredly. "And it was dark by the time we got over there. What are you worried about, Seitz?"

"A friend. Dionis Mather. She's a Tuckernuck care-taker—the one who radioed the Coast Guard tonight to report the distress flare. She hasn't made it home."

Merry let out a hiss of breath and glanced at her storm-lashed bedroom window. "That *sucks*. You think she's still on the water?"

"I hope not. I hope she's warm and dry in one of the

houses she takes care of. But Merry, tell me something."
Howie's voice grew, if possible, more strained. "Did you
find the guns?"

"I found a Glock, yeah—although *where* I found it
poses some questions."

"*It?* You only found *one?*" Seitz persisted.

"Why—are there more?" Merry frowned and sat up
higher against her pillows.

"The bullets taken from the two victims don't match.
Or so I think," Howie amended. "The State Crime Lab
will have to confirm that. But one round—in the female
victim—fragmented. The one in the male victim did not.
That suggests to me that the rounds were different. One
high velocity, the other low."

"Fired from two different guns," Merry added immediately. "Think they shot each other?"

"Not if you found only one weapon."

Her thoughts raced at Howie's implication. The bullet
that grazed Bradley Minot's scalp had traveled on through
the port window in the seating area. She suspected it was
now underwater, unrecoverable. Yet she'd found a gun
wedged between the sofa cushions. It hadn't made sense
to her at the time; the weapon ought to have been near
Bradley's hand. But if he'd been struck by a round from
a *different* gun . . . fired from several yards away . . . near
where the woman had been found . . .

Clarence had conducted the evidence collection in
that part of the yacht, and there was no one better at
searching a scene, in Merry's experience. But Clarence
had found no weapon. If the female victim had fired at
Bradley Minot, wouldn't the woman's gun have been
lying near her?

"There was a couple million dollars' worth of heroin on *Shytown*," she told Howie absently.

"Jesus." He was breathing so heavily, he sounded like he was hyperventilating. "And only *one gun*? Since when do dealers travel without an arsenal, Mer? Are you *sure* the victims were the only people on that boat?"

She thought back hurriedly to the cabins she and Clarence had searched once they'd discovered the drugs. They'd had so little time—the yacht's hull shifting on the sandbar, the storm bludgeoning them, and the chopper hovering uneasily overhead. They'd ransacked lockers in the fore and aft staterooms, looking for more plastic-wrapped kilos of heroin. Merry thought there'd been clothes and books in one of the single side cabins as well, toiletries in the bathroom nearby. At the time, neither she nor Clarence had talked about the fact that personal items were scattered all over the boat.

Items belonging to a *third person*? Or more?

"No," she told Howie. "I'm not sure."

"What if somebody escaped? Left the victims behind for the Coast Guard to find?"

And planted the gun in the cushions. Shoving it down so that even if the boat moved off the bar—even if it sank in the hurricane—the weapon might eventually be found during salvage operations. Incriminating at least one of the victims, perhaps, in a murder . . .

Merry said, "You think a killer's riding out a hurricane somewhere on Tuckernuck."

"Just like Di," Howie finished bleakly.

THE LIGHT WAS still on in the barn when she rounded the driveway of the Benson mansion. Dionis walked toward the yellow beacon slowly and painfully from the truck she'd left at the end of the drive.

She had pulled on her clothes and socks as soon as the cab door slammed shut behind her wracked body, then huddled close to the truck's heating vents until her shuddering subsided. Only then did Dionis turn the ignition and drive through the gale-force blasts toward Northern Light.

Her father's old workhorse shuddered and rocked as the storm buffeted it, fighting her grip on the wheel. Tuckernuck had few trees, none of any height to speak of, no windbreaks except the occasional house. She might as well have been churning across a tundra or desert. Dionis's headlights picked out sand clouds and bare shrubs, uprooted and bucketing along in the wind. Several struck the truck's sides, bounced off the hood. Her windshield was scoured with rain and sand. She glanced at the dashboard clock as the security gate swam into view; nearly nine-thirty. She had been gone something like an hour and a half—she couldn't entirely remember. Her brain was groggy, as though she'd been concussed. The effect, Dionis suspected, of near-hypothermia.

But she had done it: she had moored the skiff as best she could, against insane odds. She would get off this island once the storm had passed, she would head straight for the hospital, and Jack would be fine again. Triumph ballooned in Dionis's lungs. She had battled the storm and survived in a fashion to make her daddy proud. She would never tell him, of course. The truth of what she'd risked and done would terrify him. She would only tell Howie. He deserved to know how he'd ordered her back to her truck, and saved her, Dionis thought; how he'd offered her no choice but life.

Suddenly she was crying at the thought of Howie, all her fear and loneliness and physical exhaustion coalescing in the conviction that *she loved him, dammit*, and they were meant to be together.

Tears streaming down her cheeks, Dionis grasped the barn door's knob. She didn't care if Joe was dead to the world in the apartment's only bed—she would pull down some straw and sleep on the floor near the horses, with one of their blankets thrown over her.

But as Dionis stepped into the warmth and light of the stalls, she saw that Joe wasn't in bed. He was sitting in a chair he'd turned to face the door. And he had a gun trained on her chest.

WHEN THE HURRICANE now known as Teddy struck 'Sconset a little after midnight, it was a Category Three on the Saffir-Simpson scale. Wind speeds at Sankaty Head Light clocked in at 123 miles per hour, blowing shingles off of the 'Sconset Market's roof and clawing at the boarded windows of The Summer House. The hotel's beachside pool and restaurant were completely submerged. Gigantic rollers swept over Codfish Park and bit deep into the bluff beyond.

Seven miles distant, Merry Folger sat up in bed at 12:24 A.M. and felt the fury of the storm batter every window and wall around her.

"Wow," Peter muttered. "Teddy's not kidding."

She thought of Ralph and her father, John, in their bathrobes snug underground at Tattle Court. "Should we wake up the kids and get everyone into the storm cellar?"

From the opposite end of the house there was a loud bang, and then the sound of breaking glass.

"Meredith? Pete?" Hale Whitney's voice. He was running down the hall. "A tree branch just blew through our window!"

Peter swore, and threw back the bedcovers. "I knew we should have boarded this place up. At least the north side."

Merry followed him. "There'll be water damage. What do we do?"

"I'll get a tarp from the garage." He pulled open the bedroom door. Hale was standing there, his face strangely youthful without his glasses. Casey, his youngest, was shivering in her nightgown behind him, balancing on one foot.

"Merry, you and George take the kids down to the living room with their pillows and blankets," Hale said. "Peter and I will pick up the glass."

Georgiana emerged from the boys' bunkroom with Trey and Harry in tow. "Where's Madeleine?"

"Still asleep," Casey piped up.

Trey rolled his eyes. "She'd snore through 9/11."

"That's not funny, Trey," Hale said evenly. "I lost friends in the World Trade Center."

"Tell her we're all camping out, Case," George ordered. "With a fire downstairs, and everything."

"I'll hunt for the marshmallows," Merry added.

"JESUS," JOE CROAKED, dropping the gun into his lap. "It's only you."

He ran the fingers of his right hand—his good hand—through his hair. Dionis noticed, with a detachment that had nothing to do with her terrified, adrenaline-singing brain, that it looked less black in the light of the radiant heat lamps now that it was dry.

"You pulled a gun on me," she breathed. "Why?"

Joe rose deliberately, set the pistol on his chair, and walked toward her. He'd put on his damp jeans, but his chest was still bare.

Dionis backed against the barn door as though it could protect her.

"I'm sorry," he said, and looked earnestly into her eyes. "I'm *sorry*, Dionis. That was unforgivable, after all you've done. I'm afraid I haven't been completely honest with you."

She licked her lips. After being drenched for what seemed liked hours, they were suddenly dry.

"I didn't get this wound by accident," Joe said. "Somebody shot me. I was trying to take the gun out of his hand—and, well . . ."

"That's why the bullet went through your palm," she whispered.

He nodded. Reached up with his good right hand and clasped her shoulder.

Dionis flinched, and pressed back against the door. She had no reason to believe him. "Where is that guy now?"

"You're freezing." Joe's brows crinkled with concern. "What happened to you out there? Where were you?"

"Down at the lagoon. Tuckernuck's boat landing," she clarified, when he looked puzzled. Her recent sense of triumph trickled away, leaving a hollow at her core that just might fill with fear. She forced herself to sound normal. "I had to secure my skiff before the hurricane hits."

As if to echo her words, the wind screamed down on the barn's aluminum roof, shaking the rafters overhead. Afterglow whinnied and bucked in her stall. Dionis started toward the horse, but Joe still held her shoulder.

"You've got a boat?" he demanded. "*Here?*"

She nodded once. *And I almost left for home in it tonight.* "Where's the guy with the gun?"

"Could be anywhere. Still on his yacht, or wandering around this island. Why do you think I staked out the door? I thought he'd come to finish what he started."

"You didn't turn out the light. Or lock the door," Dionis said tensely. "Did you *want* him to find you?"

"Better the enemy you can see, than the one who keeps you guessing."

Hysteria frayed her voice. "Joe, what's going on? Why'd he shoot you in the first place?"

He smiled at her. And his face—she saw with that same odd detachment—was ridiculously handsome. Like something out of the movies. Everything that had happened that night was unreal.

"You need food." He released her shoulder gently. "There's soup in the kitchen. I'll tell you all about it while we open the cans."

Chapter Sixteen

THE SOUP WAS tomato. Better if they'd had cheese sandwiches, too, Dionis thought, but there was no bread, and the one piece of cheddar dying slowly in the refrigerator drawer was as stiff as plastic.

"So, this isn't your place," Joe observed as she hunted in the cupboard for a sauce pan.

"God, no." She glanced at him over her shoulder. "I'm just a caretaker. The estate belongs to Todd Benson."

"The quarterback?" Shock registered on Joe's face. "Jesus. But he's not here, right?"

"Oh, no. I told you—everybody's gone. Because of the hurricane."

Too late, she wondered if she ought to have lied. Invented a Jorie Engstrom or Brad Kramer waiting to jump out of the woodwork. But Joe hadn't picked up the gun again and his sheer normalcy, his concentration on heating soup, reassured Dionis that she was imagining menace.

"So why are you still here?" he asked. "Don't get me wrong—I'm glad I found an open door, but . . ."

"I came back over from Nantucket to check on the horses. There was a glitch getting them off."

"Nice of you."

"Stupid as hell," Dionis said bitterly. "I was supposed to make sure they were fed and watered and then get straight back home to Nantucket. My dad had a heart attack this afternoon. He's in surgery—*was* in surgery—and I have no idea if he survived. Because, no cell coverage. And now I'm stuck—"

"I'm sorry," Joe said.

Dionis nodded distractedly. She didn't underline that she would have been back at Jack Mather's bedside right now if Joe hadn't walked in out of the storm; it wasn't really his fault. Just one of those things. But . . .

"Why were you out on the water in a hurricane warning, anyway?" she demanded.

His eyebrows quirked in a way she found annoying. "Vacation cruise that ended badly. How do you evacuate an entire island?"

"One house at a time. Most of them were empty already." Dionis set the pan on the stove. Joe was good at turning the conversation from himself to her. "Tuckernuck places aren't winterized. Nobody's here year-round."

"Summer people." He smirked. "Money, huh?"

Dionis frowned. "Not really. I mean—*yes*, sure, the places are worth something, but Tuckernuck isn't upscale. It's sort of . . . *old*."

She could see he didn't understand what she meant.

"Old New England money," she attempted. "Which is the kind that doesn't advertise. The kind that's simple, and passed down—not like Long Island money. There are only about forty houses here, spread out over nine hundred acres, and they've all been owned by the same few families for the past couple of hundred years." LaFarges. Coffins. Husseys. The names were interwoven through marriages and deaths, decade after decade, and carved in the wood of Tuckernuck houses.

Joe glanced around the barn: at the rubber flooring, the radiant lamps, the gorgeousness of the horses. "This doesn't look simple. And I haven't even seen the main house."

"Oh, well, *Benson*—" Dionis halted in mid-sentence. Todd Benson was a puzzle. Nobody could explain how he'd been allowed to buy land on Tuckernuck. *Nobody* who wasn't related to the original families—or had friends, cousins, or deep influence with the homeowners association—could force their way onto the island.

"There's a reason for that," Jack Mather had explained to Dionis when she first started working with him as a caretaker, after graduate school. "Nantucket's bought and sold by the highest bidders these days. Whole nature of the island has changed since Wall Street money poured in. All those compounds? The swimming pools? Personal chefs flown in for a few weeks at a time? That'd happen on Tuckernuck, too, if you let strangers buy and build. People would pay the earth for this kind of unspoiled privacy—then they'd price everybody else out of the market. Drive away the old-timers and riffraff. Build private runways. Private restaurants and golf clubs. *Jet-setters* with shingle palaces on the beachfront, Di! They'd want a *ferry* to Madaket, for chrissake. Think about it. The old families won't let some yahoo throw down a hundred million and spoil their backyards forever."

So how had Todd Benson done it?

Northern Light had taken three summers to complete, with an architect, interior designer, and landscape architect flown in by helicopter from New York. The

Bensons hired an expensive Nantucket contractor to get their blueprints approved by the conservation board. He imported his construction crews from Hyannis. Dionis knew this because she and Jack were hired to shuttle sub-contractors and earthmovers and building supplies from Madaket in their work skiffs and barges. The crews lived in trailers on the Northern Light building site all week long. Each Friday, Dionis and Jack took them off Tucker-nuck and drove them to Ackerman Field for the trip back to Cape Cod.

"My dad says Benson got lucky," she told Joe. "A bunch of extended family inherited a house and property out here. Except none of them lived on the East Coast anymore, and the ones who wanted to keep the Tucker-nuck place couldn't buy out the others. So, they had to put it up for sale and divide the proceeds."

"That must happen a lot."

"No," Dionis countered. "It doesn't. The people who love Tuck, love it with a fierce passion that's impossible to explain. Families kill themselves to keep a foothold here. And if they can't—sometimes a group of neighbors band together to buy a property when it goes up for sale. They donate parcels to the Tuckernuck Land Trust, just to keep them off the market. They don't want outsiders. I guess Benson slipped under the radar."

"He's done that for years on the football field," Joe pointed out.

The soup was hot. Dionis ladled out two bowls and handed Joe a package of saltines she'd found in a drawer. "You're better at asking questions than answering them. But you've avoided this one long enough. Who shot you, and why?"

Joe took a sip of soup. He'd put his damp shirt back on, now, and except for the bandage on his left hand, might be any chance acquaintance sharing a meal in a hurricane.

"Where to begin," he murmured.

"With the answer?" Dionis suggested.

Joe shook his head. "It starts in Chicago, I guess. About four years ago. That's where I knew this guy. Call him . . . Matt."

"Matt," she repeated. "But that's not really his name."

Joe smiled crookedly. "It's as good as any. He's the son of a guy who made a killing on the Chicago exchange. A trust fund baby. Matt and I were fraternity brothers in college, actually. Only we went our separate ways out of school. Matt decided to see the world by boat. I went into private security."

"Private security."

Joe shrugged. "I majored in criminal investigation. Matt majored in econ. Only one of us really needed a job."

"I see."

He glanced up at her. "Sit down, Dionis. You haven't touched your soup."

She drew out the café table's second chair and perched on it. Picked up her spoon. The soup was already congealing, with the unfortunate pink skin that always scummed the top of canned tomato. "When did you move out here?"

"Last winter. Only I actually moved to St. John." Joe bit into a saltine. "That's where Matt keeps his yacht from October to May. His dad had persuaded him to hire me. As crew."

"On the boat that just grounded?"

He nodded. "*Shytown*. Named for the best city on earth. A two-year-old Hatteras 75 Panacera, for which he paid cash."

"You're shitting me." Dionis knew boats. Matt had bought a very expensive dream. "He's got that much of a trust fund?"

"Probably tapped a few million of his principal," Joe reflected, "but that was alright. His dad expected him to buy a house. Bought a house that floats, is all."

"—Except when it's stuck on a shoal in a hurricane. How'd that happen?" Dionis asked.

Joe pushed aside his soup bowl. "We got into an argument this afternoon." He was staring down at the table, his expression brooding. "Matt wanted to head straight for Long Island—he rents a slip at a marina on the North Shore during the summer. I thought it would be safer to put in at Nantucket. I was at the wheel, and Matt was below napping. But he woke up and realized we were off course. Then he pulled a gun on me."

"That's insane." Dionis looked at him wildly. No one she knew in the boat business pulled a gun on their crew. "Why?"

"I think—" Joe hesitated. "It has to do with his father. Matt thought he'd done me a favor by hiring me. But he figured out today that actually, he was set up. His old man sent me—a friend he trusted—to keep an eye on Matt. Spy on him, even, and report back. When I acted in his best interest . . . he resented it."

"But a *gun*?"

Joe grimaced. "He's not wrong to keep one on board. Pirates are a thing, Dionis—particularly in the Caribbean. Hell, I carry a weapon, as you know."

"But you're trained security! He *shot* you!"

"I'm not sure he meant to. He ordered me to head west, closer to the mainland, and then turn south for Long Island. But it was getting dark, and the storm surge forced us onto the shoals. When we grounded, Matt went nuts—*Shytown* is his world, and I'd threatened it. He came at me. I tried to take the gun away from him. It went off in my hand."

Dionis studied him, her lips parted in disbelief. "This guy is unstable."

Joe laughed abruptly. "Why do you think I jumped overboard?"

"Is he crazy enough to hunt you down?"

"I don't know." Joe spread his hands and his eyes widened, as confounded as Dionis. "Honestly? I think he'll stay with *Shytown*. The boat means more to him than I do. But when I woke up and found that you were gone . . . then heard somebody walking toward the barn . . ."

"You were ready for the worst."

"Again. I'm really sorry."

Overhead, the lights flickered and went out.

The room was filled with darkness and the shriek of the storm.

A buzzer sounded, and the lights glared on again.

"Backup generator." Dionis expelled a shaky breath. "Of course, Benson has one—or several. But I think the wind has the right idea. Let's turn out the lights, Joe. And lock the barn door."

HOWIE SEITZ SPENT most of the night dozing uncomfortably in the back of his car. The Nissan's rear seat folded down, which offered a nice square of cargo area if he needed to transport a bike, but it was insufficient for the full extent of Howie's lanky frame. He had taken to the car, which was parked in the garage beneath his apartment because one of his three windows had blown out completely, leaving glass and scraps of worn wooden molding scattered across half the room.

The half where his bed was.

Howie had wadded his comforter into a hefty plug and thrust it through the gaping window, but he knew that was a short-term solution. The plug would absorb water then deposit it all over his mattress. He didn't trust the other two windows to hold, either. He pulled the bed into the middle of the room and beat it for the garage.

He slept only fitfully, dreaming that he clawed his way up a wave that grew and grew above him, curling with menace, only to slip and tumble back down into its trough. At the wave's peak swirled a black head. A hand reaching up in supplication. *Dionis*. Drowning. *He had to reach her.*

He snorted awake in the darkness, aware that the metal panels of the garage door were shuddering in the storm's wind. *Fuck this,* he thought. He thrust himself stiffly out of the Nissan's hatch, threw up the door, and let the torrential rain scour his face. He had no idea what time it was. Where Dionis was. *God, if she was out on the water last night—*

He could not face Jack Mather in the hospital today without some answers.

Howie turned around, feeling in the pocket of his sweats for his keys. The least he could do was see whether she'd made it back to Jackson Point.

DIONIS WOKE WITH a start and a faint murmur of protest. She hated to leave the warm strength of Howie's arms, or give up the powerful sense of *home* she'd felt as he held her. The sensation was so real she looked wildly around the room as she sat up, searching for him, then realized where she was. Lying on Todd Benson's rubber barn floor, near the two palominos' stalls, wrapped in a blanket.

A persistent beating noise filled her ears, as though an angry mob was pummeling the barn walls with pitchforks. *The wind.* Alive and violent, as though it were coming personally for her. And yet somehow, Dionis had slept through the first moments as the hurricane hit. By her watch, it was 2:37 A.M.

Dad, she thought.

Was he alive? Did he know she hadn't come back to him? Could she ever forgive herself, if worry made his condition worse?

Dionis unwound herself from the blanket and, leaving the barn in darkness, crept to the main door. When she released the bolts, a world of rain and ferocity tore the door from her hand and blew it wide open.

She stood there, framed against the hurricane and the night, her black hair streaming. Her cheeks wet with rain and something else. *Oh, Daddy—please be alive.*

Behind her, Afterglow reared and screamed in her stall, her hooves striking out at the wooden walls. Dionis jumped out of her skin. She turned instantly, fighting the windblown door to close it. Once she got her shoulder against the surface she could apply her full 118 pounds and force it closed. Then she ran to the frightened animal.

"Shhhhhhh," she muttered, as Afterglow bucked and

grunted, then spun in a tight circle around her loose box. "I'm here, baby girl. I'm here. It's okay."

Behind her Honeybear snorted. His head was extended as far as possible through the notch in his stall door.

Afraid Afterglow might hurt herself battering the wall with her hooves, Dionis reached toward the shivering palomino. Her warm fingertips grazed the horse's hide in a gesture of comfort. Afterglow was streaming with moisture.

Simply opening the door for a few seconds couldn't have drenched the horse. Dionis glanced up at the barn's open-framed roof. Was it leaking? She couldn't see much in the howling dark. Should she throw on the lights and figure out what was going on? But what if the man who'd shot Joe—Matt, she remembered his name was—saw the light, and forced his way in from the storm?

The apartment door swung open. "Dionis?"

"Over here," she yelled. The wind had crescendoed like a revving jet engine, making normal conversation impossible.

Joe switched on the apartment's light. He was standing barefoot in the doorway, squinting in Dionis's direction.

The warm yellow glow was instantly comforting, whether it drew a thousand killers to the door. One decision made for her.

"What's with the horse?" he called over the wind.

"She's getting soaked. I think the roof's leaking."

Dionis crossed the barn floor and threw on the main room's master switch. Thank God for expensive backup generators. She hoped Todd Benson's tank had enough propane to get them through Teddy's worst.

Joe joined her by the mare's stall and craned his head upward. "Right there," he said, pointing to the far corner.

"There's a deluge pouring in. Looks like some of the roof has blown off."

"I didn't hear it go!"

"It's a pretty small area, along the gutter seam." He glanced at her. "You were probably asleep."

Joe certainly had been. He looked groggy.

"We should get this girl into the stall next to Honeybear," Dionis said. "I bet being closer to him would calm her."

"She's certainly not calm now." Joe looked doubtfully at the mare. "I don't want to open that door. She could kick us both down."

"I wish I knew more about horses."

At that moment, the wind dropped precipitously. And died.

The fusillade of rain pattered away, slowly and reluctantly, to nothing.

Dionis stared at Joe. The hurricane's voice still rang in her ears and skull.

"Eye of the storm," he said briefly. "Even she knows it."

Afterglow heaved a great sigh, her flanks heaving, and bobbed her head in relief.

Dionis eased the horse's hot pink halter over her ears, then opened the stall door and led her carefully out.

Joe had positioned himself by the open door of the loose box opposite, right next to Honeybear, who whickered impatiently when he saw the mare was free. Dionis led Afterglow into the dry stall.

"Toss me a towel," she ordered. "Not one of yours—there are horse towels in the feed room next door. Near the horses' shower."

Joe disappeared, then returned with a couple of

heavy-duty terrycloth rags. He handed them over the
stall door and Dionis tentatively placed one on Afterglow's back, which was dark blonde with rainwater.

She began to rub gently, afraid the horse would rear at
her touch—but Afterglow merely snatched a mouthful of
hay from the feeding bracket Dionis had filled and stood
contentedly munching while she rubbed. Encouraged,
Dionis toweled off the horse vigorously, even edging
around Afterglow's head (not her hind legs; Dionis wasn't
that confident) to dry the opposite side.

"Here's the blanket," Joe said, when she had draped
the sodden towels over the stall door.

Dionis arranged it over the horse's back and snapped
the buckles. "I should put one of these on Honeybear,
too. Just so he doesn't get jealous."

She backed out of the mare's stall and fetched another
horse blanket from the feed room. Honeybear butted her
chest with his nose when she slipped into his stall, and
she rubbed the velvet warmth. "You're such a boo," she
murmured, easing the padded cloth over his back. "I suppose you don't really need this, but let's pretend it's like
a thunder shirt for dogs. A little friendly pressure on the
spine when the elements get too hairy."

She patted the gelding's rump and left him.

"Hope the rest of the roof stays put," Joe muttered.

Dionis glanced up. Her ears were still buzzing with
remembered cacophony. "Any idea how long a hurricane
eye takes to pass?"

"Depends how large it is. And how fast the storm is
moving inland."

She checked her watch. "It's been at least fifteen minutes since the wind dropped."

"Maybe another few minutes, then, before it starts up again."

They looked at each other, holding onto the fragile peace. Dreading the moment the hurricane's outer bands fell like a judgment on their heads.

"How about a slug from that vodka bottle?" Joe suggested.

"There's actually one left?"

He brought what remained of the vodka from the bedroom, along with his comforter. Now that she had the time to look at him, Dionis didn't like what she saw. Joe's eyes were glassy, and his face was flushed.

Fever, from his wounded hand.

"You take the slug," she told him. "I'm going to make some tea."

The two of them sat up, backs against the wall, shoulders touching, waiting for the hurricane to strike again.

Chapter Seventeen

"HE'S NOT BRADLEY Minot," Howie said.

Merry had just battled her way into the station from the Fairgrounds Road parking lot, which was ankle-deep in floodwater. It was after six-thirty in the morning and the eye of the hurricane had passed over Nantucket hours before. The rain, falling from its outer bands, was still torrential. Wind speeds topped eighty miles per hour. The streets of town were submerged from the harbor all the way up to Federal, and most people were wisely staying snug inside. Unless, of course, their roofs had blown off.

Most of Old North Wharf's picturesque cottages had been reduced to matchsticks, roofs blown off, window frames sagging, and in some cases, walls collapsed. The Wharf Rats clubhouse, Merry saw with a pang, was completely trashed and standing in seawater. The shops and restaurants on Straight Wharf had been similarly abused, with the added indignity of powerboats blown straight through their guts—the boats having been tossed onto the pier by storm surge.

Great Harbor Yacht Club's pilings were strewn with the hulls of dinghies and small sailboats that hadn't made it out of the water. Masts of submerged sailing vessels stabbed forlornly and drunkenly from beneath the Boat Basin's waters.

Abandoned cars, flooded to their roofs, formed artificial reefs along the side streets.

Merry bit her inner cheek in dismay as she descended from the relative protection of Cliff Road's height to the flooded mess of town. It would be weeks—*months*—before Nantucket could drag itself out of waist-high debris. The insurance claims would be enormous, given the wind and water damage to expensive historic homes, the sodden inventories of countless high-end stores. Murray's Toggery Shop and Mitchell's Book Corner looked undamaged on the upper end of Main. Nantucket Bookworks and the Jared Coffin House on Broad Street would survive, although a tree had crashed across the Coffin House's slate terrace—

Three more ancient trees, whose roots had heaved and clawed the cobblestones of upper Main since the whaling age, had been thrown down in ruin like deposed kings. A crew from the town's Department of Public Works was already attempting to clear the mess with power saws and a truck-bound crane, but the street was still impassible. Merry turned her SUV and backtracked to Orange, which was clear out to The Rotary.

Now, safely inside the station, she reflected that it was good that her father, while chief, had spearheaded the police department's move to Fairgrounds Road. The old station she'd known and loved as a child, where Ralph Waldo had ruled on Water Street, was undoubtedly flooded. This larger, newer, and more sophisticated headquarters was clearly operating on backup generator power at the moment, but at least it was dry. They had enough propane in the backup tanks to keep the station running for a week.

Merry lifted her hood and accepted the cup of coffee Howie offered her. "Who is he, then?"

"No idea. But the New York driver's license in that wallet the Coast Guard found is fake."

"Not surprising, I guess, given the drugs and guns." Merry sipped her coffee gratefully; she was feeling the effects of a broken night spent on the living room's sisal. "Does the ID picture match the male victim's face?"

"From what I could glimpse around all the bandages? Hard to tell. His eyes are closed."

"Anything else in the wallet?"

"Three credit cards, one of them black."

"Ah," Merry said. "A high-credit individual. I thought drug people dealt in cash."

Howie shrugged. "If you're moving around boat slips up and down the coast, you've got to have some way to reserve online, right?"

"All the cards have the name Minot on them, I suppose?"

By way of answer, the sergeant fanned them under her nose.

"Which means," Merry said as she scanned them, "he committed fraud correctly. He backstopped it with a stolen social security number."

"Pulled from the records of somebody who's dead."

"Did you take his prints last night?"

"Yeah. I submitted them to the MBI for IAFAS search this morning, but the results aren't back yet."

Howie was referring to the FBI's Integrated Automated Fingerprint Identification System. This is the national database of all fingerprints and criminal histories, which the bureau's Criminal Justice Information System maintains. The Nantucket Police electronically sends sets of fingerprints taken as evidence to the Massachusetts Bureau of Investigation, which then submits them to the IAFAS database. The search response—meaning, an identified print match, or no—usually comes back within hours. But that would require the MBI to be up and running at full capacity today. And Merry knew the Massachusetts bureau was subject to the same weather—and personnel shortages—as Nantucket.

Prints remained their best hope of identifying the comatose victim. The IAFAS database held some sixty million criminal histories; it received over one hundred thousand fingerprint submissions daily.

"You submitted the female victim's, too?" Merry asked.

"Of course."

The physical evidence her team had collected—ballistics, fibers, blood samples—could not be sent out to MBI for forensic analysis until the weather improved. Nantucket would be cut off from the mainland by air and sea for at least another twenty-four hours, Merry guessed. Longer, if the island's airport or ferry terminals had sustained significant damage. Hurricane Teddy was battering the Cape and Boston, too; and it would move further inland over the next hours and days. Which meant it was anyone's guess when the fingerprint evidence would be logged at MBI.

The police department was sitting on a fortune in heroin, she thought uneasily, with no way to ship it out. But storm or no storm, they'd have to do what they could with the evidence at hand.

"Walk with me, Seitz." Merry led the sergeant back toward her desk. "Clarence found the woman's purse last night. While I'm typing up my report for Pocock, you figure out whether *her* ID is fake, too."

THE CHIEF, AS it happened, wasn't in the Nantucket Police station to receive Merry's report that morning; he was at a crisis meeting with the Fire Department chief, the head of Public Works, the Coast Guard and his emergency management coordinator, Scott Tredlow.

A few minutes after 8 A.M., Pocock called in to the department phone sitting on Merry's desk.

"I have no record of you opening a murder investigation in the past twelve hours, detective," he said by way of greeting, "and none at all of a heroin bust. What the hell were you doing last night? Celebrating your marriage vows early?"

Merry felt her eyebrows soar in shock, then closed her eyes in resignation. Of *course* Pocock would behave like a putz. Never mind that she'd risked her life, Clarence's life, the Coast Guard Jayhawk crew . . . to secure evidence that by now would otherwise have been at the bottom of the sound.

"I'm typing up my initial report as we speak, chief."

"Too bad you didn't do that yesterday. I suppose you were too busy choosing place settings to bother sharing your news. Do you have any *idea* how bush-league it feels, how *fucking embarrassing* it is, to learn about this from the *Coast Guard*? Jesus. The Coast Guard! A bunch of guys too unqualified for the Navy."

Thinking of Terry and Farmer and Natalie O'Neill, Merry stifled a furious response. "We owe the Joint Air

Station crew our gratitude, sir, for making the evidence collection—and the heroin haul—possible. They risked their lives." She didn't bother to mention that she and Clarence had, too; the chief would say that he expected no less.

"Don't tell me about the Nantucket Police Department's *debts*, detective," Pocock seethed. "We're so in the red right now we have to share *credit* for the drug seizure with the rest of the known goddamn world! I hold you responsible."

If that meant she got to pose with Bruce Farmer and Natalie and Clarence for press pictures, Merry would gladly take responsibility. But knowing Pocock, he'd be the only man at the podium when the heroin find was announced.

"You've ID'd the perps, I hope," he snarled into her ear.

Interesting word choice, Merry thought. She'd have used the word *victims* herself, as she still didn't know who owned the gun. But Pocock would view everybody on *Shytown* as drug mules. "We're working on it, sir. At least one was operating under an alias."

"And the other?"

"The deceased victim. Female. A resident of New York, from her identification. We've established it's valid. We're trying to locate next of kin."

"I want that report in the next fifteen minutes."

It would be incomplete, then, but—*whatever*.

"Yes, sir."

Merry cradled the receiver, dial tone already singing.

ASHLEY RUSSO, SHE typed into her computer, and attached the photograph of the female victim scanned from her driver's license. *Thirty-two years old, licensed childcare provider in the State of Illinois, currently resident in Islip, New York. Employed as a bartender at Glen Cove Marina.*

Howie had discovered this much in his background check on the dead woman. He had also put a name to her next of kin: Ashley's mother, Lorraine Russo, who appeared to live alone in the Elmwood Park section of Chicago.

Merry spared a few moments to think of Lorraine, whom she would have to interview by phone once the local police had rung the woman's doorbell and broken the news of her daughter's death. Merry had sent out the next-of-kin notification request to the Elmwood Park precinct, and was hoping for confirmation soon. Nobody liked to give that kind of news over the phone; when possible, it was done in person. Merry was relieved that for once she didn't have to do it.

She hated breaking the news of violent death. She had lost too many people of her own. But it was that visceral knowledge of grief that compelled her to show up at her desk every day—to put a name to killers—and assign blame for the misery they caused.

Would Lorraine give a good goddamn about any of that? No. After the local police left her numb, she'd stumble upstairs to the closet where she kept Ashley's kindergarten drawings, her much-loved stuffed animals, the dress she'd worn to her sophomore high school winter ball—and bury her nose in the lingering trace of her daughter's irreplaceable, indescribable scent.

Lorraine would never empty the closet. She would never wash those clothes.

Who had Ashley Russo been, Merry wondered? How had the bartender ended up on a drug-dealer's yacht, with her gut torn apart by a fragmenting bullet? Merry had looked at the woman's dead face in Cottage Hospital. The beginning of marionette lines ran from her nose to mouth, and there were crow's feet at the corners of her eyes. Her clothes were neither flashy nor shabby, her jewelry minimal. Had Ashley been friends with the man lying in a coma, who was *not* named Bradley Minot? Did she know his real name? Were they lovers? Enemies? And who, exactly, had tried to kill whom?

Howie's words from the previous night echoed through Merry's mind. *Are you sure the victims were the only people on that boat?* No. She wasn't sure of anything. Maybe Bradley-not-Minot and Ashley Russo had killed each other. Maybe one had tried to commit suicide. Or maybe they had both been shot by someone else. Why, then, the fake ID and credit cards in not-Minot's wallet?

The report she sent Bob Pocock held more questions than answers. Somebody else, Merry reasoned, would have to unravel the mess. She'd be in Europe in a few days' time, when the investigation was fully underway, blissfully sipping Bordeaux and staring out over the Seine. One of her colleagues would tell her what really went down on *Shytown* the night Teddy hit, once her honeymoon was over.

Forgive me, Peter, Meredith thought, *for hating that.*

HOWIE CHECKED HIS email for a response to his IAFAS query. But in his heart, he knew it was too soon, given the hurricane hitting all of New England. The Massachusetts Bureau of Investigation might even be

closed today. He stretched his arms over his head, yawning. Then, restless as hell, Howie wandered over to the
coffee station to refill his mug. *Dionis.* Where was she?
What had happened to her? He'd driven out again to
Madaket this morning, parking his car well before Ames
Avenue and the flooded bridge to Jackson Point, surging
through seawater above his knees. He'd stood where the
lot used to be, water up to the fenders of cars and the hulls
of trailered boats, his shoulders hunched against the rain,
and waited for first light. But Di's skiff hadn't miraculously
reappeared, and her father's truck hadn't been moved—as
it might have, if she'd made it home. Nothing about Jackson Point had changed, except the depth of the water
crashing over the submerged dock.

Howie glanced around the room. Every single officer
had reported for duty this morning, whether scheduled
or not. Once Pocock returned from his interdepartmental crisis meeting, every breathing soul on the Nantucket
Police would be sent out on disaster relief. Howie would
be directing traffic or checking on emergency rescue calls
from Tom Nevers and Surfside. He might not get this
chance for the rest of the day.

He picked up his phone and dialed the number he now
knew by heart.

"Howie!" Terry Samson crowed. "You still breathing?"

"Barely. You?"

"Brant Point is under four feet of water, cresting at
eight with every wave," he said. "The Boat Basin is an
unholy mess and there are hulls six deep on Children's
Beach. What can I do for you?"

"Just checking in to see whether you've pulled the reg-
istration info on that yacht. *Shytown.*"

"I have, indeed." Howie heard Terry shifting paper. "It's registered under the Bahamian flag to an LLC entitled Windy City Investments. It was most recently berthed at Glen Cove Marina."

"Thanks, Terry—I'll pass that on to Meredith."

"I'm sure she's got her hands full with this storm."

"Yeah," Howie agreed. "Did you get a lot of distress calls overnight? From out on the water?"

"We logged about two dozen up and down the Cape and Islands District, but if you're asking about Dionis Mather, she wasn't one of them. She knows how to use the VHF, Howie."

Unless it was disabled. Or Dionis was dead.

Howie chewed his lip. "How soon before it's safe to get a boat over to Tuckernuck?"

"God, I don't know," Terry sighed. "We'd have to have a good reason. Can't usually send a response boat in there, because of the shoals."

"Doesn't the storm surge mean the waters around Tuck are deeper right now? Wouldn't that help your draught?"

"Maybe," Terry agreed grudgingly, "but I can't prioritize my crews in that direction unless there's an emergency. We've got too many other claims on our time."

Howie kicked his chair back on its hind legs in frustration. He couldn't prove a crisis; Dionis might be anywhere. The fact she was last known to be headed for Tuckernuck didn't *prove* an emergency. "What about the crime scene Detective Folger boarded last night?"

"The grounded yacht?" Terry paused. Howie could hear him thinking.

"Guns and drugs, Terry. A lot more evidence to be

collected, on both our parts. It'd be good to know if the boat's still there—or sunk, or adrift."

"True."

"Chief's about to announce a heroin seizure with good press for the Coast Guard. Be a little odd if we have to admit we lost the vessel."

Howie waited as Terry's sleep-deprived mind percolated its thoughts.

"Tell you what," the Coast Guard chief said. "There's an HC-144 crew out of Joint Air Base Cape Cod scheduled for general overflight about thirteen hundred hours. I'll request an aerial search of yesterday's grounding site. Tell them to keep an eye out for any vessel adrift in the area that matches the Hatteras's description. Then at least we can say we're on it."

"Tell them to check for survivors on Tuckernuck, too."

"Jack Mather's girl?" Terry asked.

"And a possible killer," Howie replied. "We think somebody ran from *Shytown* last night."

Chapter Eighteen

"Ms. Russo?" Merry had closed her door and opened her laptop. She hoped the victim's mother wouldn't be put off by the sound of a keyboard as they spoke. "This is Detective Meredith Folger of the Nantucket Police. I'm investigating your daughter Ashley's death. Would you have a few moments to speak with me?"

"They said you'd call," Lorraine Russo breathed. Her voice was ragged and high, a voice drained from sobbing. "That's the only reason I answered the phone."

"I am so dreadfully sorry for your loss, Ms. Russo," Merry attempted.

"You didn't know her."

"No, ma'am, I did not. But I intend to find out what happened to her."

"That won't bring her back."

"No, ma'am. And it will not lessen your grief one iota. But hunting for the truth is my job. It might help *you* to help me. Give you a way to fight back against what happened to your daughter."

She had learned from raw experience how to talk to survivors. Most were desperate to vent their grief and anger, and the police—who had simultaneously failed to save a beloved person *and* delivered the dreadful news of death—were the obvious people to abuse. Merry tried to meet the grieving halfway. *I'm going to cause you pain. And I can't resurrect the dead. But if you talk to me, you may feel less helpless.*

Lorraine's voice rose an octave in frustration. "I don't even know why she was on that boat!"

"Neither do we. Did Ashley ever mention a friend who took her out in his yacht?"

"She didn't know those kinds of people!"

Except obviously, she had.

Merry waited for the woman on the other end of the line to draw breath.

"Ashley was down-to-earth," Lorraine attempted. "Practical. She was careful with her money and the way she spent her time. I can't imagine her walking off the job without telling anybody."

"Are you aware we found a significant amount of illegal heroin in the boat's hold?"

Lorraine gasped. News of the drug bust had *not* been part of the precinct's briefing.

"She had nothing to do with that!" the woman cried. "Ashley would never . . . Is that why they shot her?"

"They?"

"Whoever killed her!"

"Anything is possible," Merry conceded. "We have so little information about what happened at this point. If you could answer my questions, we'll have a better chance of establishing the truth."

"My girl was *not* mixed up with drugs," Lorraine declared. "I'll tell you anything you need to know."

Merry poised her fingers over her keyboard. "How long ago did Ashley leave the Chicago area, Ms. Russo?"

"This past spring."

"So . . . March? May?"

"Mid-April or so. She thought she'd job hunt for the fall school year—Ashley's a teacher—but it turns out she was too late. She could only get a substitute-teacher slot. And she took a summer job bartending, to pay rent." Lorraine paused. "I hated that. I didn't send her to college to tend bar."

I can't imagine her walking off the job . . .

Except, again, she already had.

"She left her teaching position in Chicago before the end of the school year? Why, Ms. Russo?"

"She was in love. Or so she said. I think she just wanted to get married—Ash's clock was ticking and she'd decided to settle for the guy next door. Only he'd moved to the East Coast by the time she finally noticed him."

"She followed a partner?" Merry's skin tingled. An unknown man might have led Ashley Russo anywhere—onto a boat full of drugs, into the path of a bullet.

"At first—but then everything fell through."

"What happened, Ms. Russo?"

"I think she decided she needed more time. Marriage is a big decision."

"It is." Merry dodged a sudden thought of her own looming wedding, and asked, "Had Ashley met someone else?"

"Not specifically, that I heard—but she was very popular with the regulars at Glen Cove. The place was filled with celebrities, she said. Very upscale."

She didn't know those kinds of people . . .

"I think she was a little dazzled," Lorraine concluded. "Thought she could do better than Kevin."

"Kevin?" Merry repeated. *Not* the name Ashley Russo had gasped as she died. That had been *Matt*.

"Kevin Monaghan. The Boy Next Door. Grew up right here in Elmwood Park, went to the same high school. I've got to tell him the news, God help me. It'll kill him."

"I see." Merry typed the name *Kevin Monaghan* into her file.

"I wanted Ash to come home when she and Kev broke up," Lorraine said wistfully, "but Ash said she really liked her apartment and the job at the marina—Glen Cove, where she worked. She decided to stay on for the fall. See if maybe a teaching job came through."

"Did she ever mention someone named Matt?"

"Matt. I don't think so. What's his last name?"

"I wish I knew." He might, Merry thought, be the person lying in Bradley Minot's hospital bed. "Do you have Kevin Monaghan's contact information, Ms. Russo? I'd like to interview him as well."

The man might know whom Ashley had been seeing in recent weeks—and who owned the boats she frequented.

Lorraine Russo gave her a number, with a New York area code.

"Did you notice any change in Ashley's life or habits—any change in her mood in recent weeks?" Merry asked.

"None."

"She didn't express any fears, or any hopes, even, about her life?"

"Just that she liked living near the sea." Lorraine was fighting tears again, her throat constricted. "What a sick joke! The sea killed her. I always tried to keep her safe. From the time she was a baby. *I kept her safe*. That was my job."

"I know, ma'am." Merry wished she could touch the bereaved woman.

"I wish she'd never moved to New York. They call Chicago a crime city, but it's got nothing on Long Island."

DIONIS WOKE TO find that she was lying slumped against Joe's right shoulder. Her cheek was damp with sweat from the heat radiating through his shirt.

She sat up and scrabbled her hair out of her eyes. Studied his face, which was flushed, and his mouth—which was slack and open. She placed her hand on his forehead. Feverish.

He opened his eyes and met her gaze, faintly questioning.

"Just checking your temp," she explained bluntly. "I'm worried your hand might be infected."

He tried to flex his bandaged fingers, and failed. "It feels swollen."

"We've got to get you to a doctor."

"Soon," he said, glancing around the barn. "The wind's not as high, you notice?"

He was right, Dionis thought. The hurricane that had battered them for the past eight hours must be moving slowly west, toward the mainland, and that thought stirred hope like breath in her lungs, for the first time since she'd left her father in Nantucket Cottage Hospital.

"We should move into the other room." She pointed to a pool of water seeping from beneath Afterglow's old stall. The rain pouring in through the hole in the roof had saturated the straw bedding and was advancing into the main barn. Fortunately, there was a drain hole in the center of the rubber floor—probably designed for hosing down the area. The horses' feet would stay fairly dry. "I'll see if there's any coffee."

"See if there's any bread," Joe suggested.

If he was hungry, he couldn't be *too* sick. "Mandy strikes me as a gluten-free kind of girl," Dionis tossed over her shoulder, "but I'll see what I can find."

There was a bag of ground coffee in the freezer, and three eggs left in the fridge. Dionis scrambled these while the coffee brewed, and put them on a plate for Joe. She was hollow from hunger, but the palominos couldn't wait; she took the pitchfork and broke off another square of hay for each of them. Honeybear nudged her affectionately as she moved past him to stuff fodder in his feeding bracket. Dionis wondered: was the horse getting cramped from lack of exercise? Should she turn him and Afterglow into the adjoining paddock in their snug blankets, once the rain began to lessen?

"I am clueless about these beasts," she sighed fretfully. "My ignorance could kill them."

His mouth full of egg, Joe shrugged. "It's not like they're going to make it anyway. I mean, you're not staying here, right? Once you get off this godforsaken island, it'll be days before somebody checks on them. Hell, if it'd been my dad in the OR, I'd have told Benson he could save his own horses."

His indifference chilled her. The palominos' beauty—their obvious emotions of fear, hunger, contentment, their intelligent eyes and unquestioning trust—had already won Dionis's heart. Joe's attitude was like a soldier of fortune's, taking what he needed to survive without remorse.

"Actually, I did this for my dad," she faltered. "Because he asked. But also because that's what caretakers *do*."

"You've certainly taken care of me," Joe replied with a crooked grin. "I'm grateful. Eat something."

The eggs were gone. Dionis scrounged in the cupboards; there were crackers, soggy with humidity. She ate these standing up, with her coffee. Black.

She had taken care of a complete stranger. While her father could be dead—or dying.

She reached for her sweatshirt. "I'm going to walk down to my truck."

"Why?" Joe said. "You can't drive off this place."

She glanced at him. "No, but I can check on my boat. And search from the road for a spot of cell phone coverage."

"Who do you plan to call, Dionis?"

His was voice was even and quiet, but irritation flared in her chest all the same.

"Nantucket Cottage Hospital."

He nodded once, looked away from the pain written on her face. "I think I can pull myself over that gate with one hand, if you help. I'll come with you."

MERRY SAT BACK in her desk chair and reached mechanically for her coffee cup, her eyes fixed unseeing on her screen. She had not reopened her office door, although most of the police station—with the exception of 911 dispatch, where phones were ringing off the hook and radio calls were incessant—was now empty and quiet. The bulk of the force was out on the road, braving the hurricane to save lives. Trees had fallen on the roofs of buildings and on parked cars. Power lines all over the island were down. A beach house under construction in Tom Nevers had been completely destroyed and washed out to sea, the bluff beneath its foundation eroded away and massive chunks of concrete and steel I-beams tumbled like a giant's Tinkertoys on the sand. But Merry had stayed quietly in her office and ignored a string of emails, intent upon following a trail so elusive she was afraid she'd completely made it up.

She had plugged Ashley Russo's name into a background database, and found little of interest. Her educational record—high school diploma and education degree from a community college. Street addresses in Elmwood Park, and briefly, in Evanston, where Ashley had worked for a year as a live-in nanny. The name of her former preschool employer and Glen Cove Yacht Club. Financial records—Ashley had never been bankrupt—and driving records. She'd paid seven traffic tickets over the years, caused one fender bender, and had been cited twice for speeding.

There were no criminal records for Ashley.

Merry ran a similar background check on Kevin Monaghan, figuring she ought to know as much as possible about the guy before she spoke with him. The results were much like Ashley's: an unimpeachable life. Kevin had gone to the same high school as the girl he'd almost married, and had once lived—as a dependent in his parents' household—on the same street as Lorraine Russo. He really was the boy next door, Merry thought. At the moment Kevin's address was listed as a town on Long Island; he held a license from the state of New York, and certification of training, as a security guard.

Merry picked up her desk phone and punched in the number Lorraine Russo had given her.

The call went straight to voicemail.

There could be multiple reasons for this, Merry considered as she placed the receiver back in its cradle. Kevin might not be able to answer calls while working his security guard job. Or he might have left his phone on its charger. Or he never picked up unidentified callers . . .

Or Kevin is lying comatose in Nantucket Cottage Hospital, Merry thought, *mistakenly identified as Bradley Minot.*

She pulled open her door and called out, "Seitz!"

Caitlyn Marshall, the duty officer on the front reception desk, turned her head. "Howie's evacuating an elderly couple from Codfish Park, Mer," she said.

She would have to wait to learn if the IAFAS database had a match for their fingerprints. But there was another possibility open to her. At Cottage Hospital.

Merry grabbed her shoulder bag and headed for the door.

"DO YOU REMEMBER roughly where your boat grounded last night?" Dionis asked as her truck lurched through the driving rain. Northern Light sat at the end of an unnamed sandy dirt road, now rutted and sodden, that required her to drive due south before she could turn east on another unpaved track and then southeast toward the lagoon.

Joe shook his head. "I have no idea. I've never been here before, remember?"

"It must have been the northern side of the island," Dionis attempted, "because I saw your distress rocket go up when I came in to the dock."

"You saw the rocket?" Joe's eyes narrowed, and his fingers, which had been attempting to pull up coverage on her cell phone, momentarily stilled.

"Uh, *yeah*," Dionis chortled. "Anybody for miles could've seen it. But I'm the one who reported it to the Coast Guard."

"Jesus *Christ*," Joe burst out. "You *reported* it?"

"What else was I supposed to do?" She shot him a glance of surprise, apprehension sparking in her brain. "That's a seaman's first duty. See a distress signal, you pick up your VHF channel."

Joe slammed her phone down on the truck's middle console with barely contained violence. "You *called the Coast Guard* last night. Before I ever found you."

Dionis flinched, her eyes trained on the streaming windshield. "Yes. Don't thank me."

"I won't! Do you *know* what you could have done? If they'd responded?"

He is out of his mind. He fired the rocket, right? "Save your sorry ass?" she suggested.

"Just don't meddle in things that aren't your business!"

"Then don't signal distress!"

"I didn't," Joe said bitterly.

Ah. So it was the guy who shot him—Matt, wasn't it?—who'd done that, she thought. There was much more to this story than Joe was telling. Dionis felt chilled.

"I bet your yacht went aground somewhere between Benson's house and East Pond," she said evenly. "We can head that way right now and see if it's still there. Although I suspect the storm surge washed it adrift."

Joe threw up his hands as though he were dealing with an imbecile. "Too dangerous."

Dionis glanced at him. Then at his remaining good hand, clenched on her Android. Matt was worrying her, again. In her restless desire to know what was happening to her father, Dionis had almost forgotten there was some-one else to be afraid of. "Even for a Hatteras Panacera?"

"You forget." He stared straight ahead. "Not my boat."

"*Not my monkeys,*" Dionis whispered under her breath. She turned left onto the main road leading to the boat landing and held out her hand. "Give me my phone."

He hesitated, then handed it to her.

She rolled down her window and thrust it out into the pounding rain. "This model's supposed to be waterproof. Let's hope they're not lying."

"Sticking it outside doesn't give you bars," he pro-tested. "There's no coverage here!"

"You never know."

Arm aloft, Dionis swept her gaze across the huddled and shrunken black oaks that lined either side of the road, barely twelve feet high and weathered from the relentless winds that scoured Tuckernuck all year. Then a differ-ent sound hit her ears, decibels beneath the hurricane's whine. She slowed the truck, pulled her hand back inside the cab, and came to a dead stop.

"What is it?" Joe demanded. He grabbed her cell from her hand. "You find coverage?"

"Nope." Dionis thrust open her truck door and stepped out into the rain. "I found the Coast Guard."

It wasn't a Jayhawk helicopter this time, but a fixed-wing aircraft emblazoned with the distinctive wide red Coast Guard stripes. It soared low overhead, oblivious to them, but Dionis began to wave frantically, jumping up and down in the road. She knew that both she and her truck were barely visible against the monochromatic, storm-lashed landscape.

"Hey! Over here!!"

The plane bore away from them, toward East Pond and the island's northern coast.

"Quick." She climbed urgently back into the cab. "We'll be too late."

As her hand reached to turn the ignition, Joe clamped down on it firmly. "What the hell are you doing?"

"It's an overflight," she rasped. "They're *looking for your yacht*. If we can get over to the north side in time, they'll know we're here!"

"No," he said.

"*What?*" She stared at him incredulously.

"We can't go anywhere near the grounding." Joe's voice was taut with strain. "Show ourselves to the plane— and we *betray* ourselves. Then it's *hunting time*. We'll be tracked down and killed before the Coast Guard, or any-one else, has the chance to save us."

Dionis stared at him wordlessly, all the fight draining from her body. Joe's dark eyes were fixed on hers and his brows were drawn down. *Warrior face*, she thought, feel-ing numbed to her toes. *He really believes it.*

"What did you do to this guy, that he wants you dead?"

"I took his girl." With his good hand, he drew his gun out of his windbreaker. Of course he had brought it. "Let's check on your boat. That's what we came out here for, isn't it?"

Chapter Nineteen

SUMMER HUGHES WAS studying Bradley Minot's chart when Merry walked into the patient's room at Cottage Hospital. The doctor looked weary and stretched around the eyes, and Merry wondered if she'd gone home during the hurricane, or simply stayed on duty. The hum of electronics and the rustle of turning pages were the only sounds, and the light was flat and gray, as though the patient's coma had seeped in like dusk to fill the space around him.

"How's he doing?" Merry asked as Summer looked up.

"Holding his own."

"What does that mean?"

"His brain swelling hasn't increased—but it hasn't disappeared entirely, either." Summer grimaced. "I've got a tentative Flight for Life from Mass Gen booked for four P.M. this afternoon—fingers crossed the storm has passed Boston by then."

Merry had caught a weather report on her way to the hospital. "They've downgraded Teddy to a tropical storm, now that it's well over the mainland," she told Summer. "I think you should be good."

She approached the bed. Summer set down the chart and came to join her. "Were you hoping he'd be conscious, so you could question him?"

"Of course. That job is going to have to be delegated to a police officer in Boston now—if this guy survives."

"I'm sorry," the doctor said. "But in a way . . . you're getting married in two days, Mer. Be grateful you can pass this one on."

"Her name was Ashley," Merry murmured.

"I'm sorry?"

"The female victim. The body you'll be sending to the Cape for autopsy as soon as the storm moves. I talked to her mom today."

"Oh, God." Summer rubbed her forehead fretfully. "That can't have been easy."

"It sucked," Merry agreed. "But that's not what I hate about my job. I hate not *seeing it through*."

She drew her cell phone out of her bag and hit redial on the number Lorraine Russo had given her for Kevin Monaghan. Justin Timberlake's "Cry Me a River" spiraled through the hospital room.

"Somebody keeps calling his cell phone," Summer remarked. "It's in that plastic bag, with the rest of his stuff. I'm surprised it hasn't run out of battery by now."

"One question answered." Merry ended the call. "We know his name is Kevin."

IT HAD TAKEN Howie too much time and patience to persuade Jean Phinney, the octogenarian owner of a cottage in Codfish Park, to leave her flooded one-story home. Her even older brother, Hugh, dressed in a pair of scalloping waders and a swordfishing cap with the bill pulled low over his brow, had greeted Howie on what had once been the lawn. Hugh was salvaging pickets floating out to sea from the Phinneys' fence, and barely stopped to wave. Howie had taken a gray Nantucket Police SUV on his mission of mercy, and its clearance allowed him to ford past the older man through the brackish sea that covered the drive. But Jean did not meet him with open arms.

"Better late than never, I guess," she said ungraciously through the six-inch gap she'd opened between herself and her storm door. "Not that I'm going with you, mind. Hurricane's over."

Knee-deep in water, Howie looked past her shoulder at the swimming main floor. "Do you have a generator, ma'am?"

"No. But I've got a camp stove. And a broom to sweep the mess out the back door."

It would take days, Howie suspected, before the flood receded and all the island's downed power lines were up and running. He offered these opinions to Jean. She disagreed. He suggested she might be warmer and more comfortable at the Red Cross shelter set up in the high school, and she laughed in his face. Jean suggested that her brother Hugh might have to call his good friend Chief Folger, and inform him that one of his cops had gone crazy. Howie politely mentioned that John Folger had been retired for over a year.

He was about to threaten to arrest both Phinneys when Hugh suddenly barked out an order to stop making the boy's life a misery and pack a clean pair of drawers. Without another word, Jean shut the door in Howie's face.

Twenty minutes later, he carted Hugh and Jean's luggage, along with Jean's cat in a pet carrier, safely into the high school. Receiving no thanks, he beat a hasty retreat and sat motionless for a few seconds behind the SUV's wheel, listening to the rain patter on the windshield. He realized something suddenly: the battering winds had dropped.

The storm was passing.

He almost drove immediately to Jackson Point, but instead, turned his car toward downtown. The winds had dropped. Terry and the Coast Guard might have some news.

SUMMER HUGHES WALKED Merry out to the inpatient floor's reception desk and hugged her goodbye. "I can't wait to see you in Mayling Stern couture on Saturday," she said. "Get some rest before then, okay?"

"You, too," Merry said. "You've been here too long."

Summer sighed. "It's unbelievable how many critical cases we've had. Low pressure induces labor, you know—we've had two C-sections in the past twenty-four hours—and then there's the cardiac patient who came in yesterday afternoon. We still haven't reached his daughter."

Merry's forehead crinkled. Seitz's friend, with the dad who'd had a heart attack. Merry knew if something similar had happened to her own father or Ralph Waldo she'd have been sick with worry, not persistently out of reach. Seitz must be right—the girl was either drowned or marooned on Tuckernuck.

Possibly with a trigger-happy refugee from *Shytown* in her neighborhood.

"Can I see your patient?"

"Jack Mather?" Summer shrugged. "I don't know why not. He's been upgraded from critical to fair condition."

Merry followed her down a different corridor. Jack Mather's eyes were closed and his pallor was yellowish—probably from opioids, Merry thought—but when the doctor entered the room, he roused himself and lifted a hand in greeting.

Summer grasped his wrist and silently assessed his pulse. "Who's this?" he asked, with a nod at Merry.

She stepped closer to the man's bedside. "Mr. Mather, I'm Detective Meredith Folger of the Nantucket Police."

His expression cleared. "John's girl."

"Yes. You know my father?"

"Who doesn't? He's a Wharf Rat. So'm I. Although your grandpa's the better storyteller." The Wharf Rats and their small shingle clubhouse on Old North Wharf were Nantucket's oldest group of friends. They gathered for coffee and conversation on almost a daily basis—although at the moment, Old North was awash, like the rest of the wharf area.

"I agree," Merry said, "but don't tell Dad I betrayed him. I understand the hospital is having a hard time reaching your daughter."

Distress flickered in Jack Mather's eyes. "No news of Dionis? You haven't . . . found her boat?"

Merry shook her head. "We can't formally look for her, either, unless you file a missing persons report. Would you like to do that, Mr. Mather?"

"Yes," he said decisively. "Anything you want. Just send out the force and find my girl. She's somewhere between Madaket and the Benson place on Tuckernuck, and she must be in trouble. It's not like Di to disappear without a word."

"That's what Sergeant Seitz told me."

"Howie." Jack's smile was shaky. "He's probably worried sick. He loves her, you know."

Merry's brows rose. "I didn't."

"With Di," Jack said, "it's impossible to do anything else."

BRANT POINT WAS under four feet of water, and the hedges of Hulbert Avenue's gracious houses had rusted startlingly brown from exposure to windblown salt water. Howie drove as far as he could down Easton Street, then abandoned the SUV and walked the final hundred yards to the Coast Guard compound's security gate, where he flashed his badge at the boatswain's mate on duty and sloshed up the steps to the Watchstanders Command Center.

Terry's sunglasses—Howie had never seen the master chief boatswain's mate without them—were pushed high on his head, and a radio transmitter was in his hand. He was staring through the station's plate glass windows at a Coast Guard response boat navigating among the vessels half sunk at their moorings in the harbor. Everything about Terry's taut frame exuded excitement; he was thriving on coffee, lack of sleep, and crisis.

"Seitz!" He slapped Howie on the back. "How the hell are you?"

"Okay," Howie replied. "I was passing by and thought I'd check in. Did anyone overfly the *Shytown?*"

"C'mere." Terry handed the transmitter to a subordinate officer and led Howie deeper into the station. "Pull up a chair. The HC-144 took aerial video footage. Man, is Tuckernuck desolate this time of year."

Howie leaned over Terry's shoulder and stared at his computer screen. The whole outline of the smaller island Dionis knew so well, smudged with rain, came up before him. The plane had approached from Martha's Vineyard and dropped in altitude as it reached Tuckernuck. First, the curving arm of the peninsular beach that guarded North Pond like a jetty. The wet charcoal gray roofs of a few buildings on the hilltop above. No boats visible on North Pond; no signs of life on the broad white ribbon of sandy road that led from it, deeper into the island.

The plane's camera followed the road east, jumping erratically as wind gusts tossed the HC-144's fuselage. The Coast Guard kept to Tuckernuck's spine, cutting straight down the center of the island, hiccupping over occasional clearings in the dense heathland of stunted black oak, pitch pine, bayberry, and shadbush. Houses stood in the clearings, along with outbuildings that probably stored generators. Roof shingles littered the ground near their foundations, along with the occasional shutter. One house—Howie hoped unloved—seemed to have burst like a papier-mâché piñata. Its roof was scattered at the crumbled feet of its walls, the home's bowels exposed to the sky. A golf cart lay like a squashed bug beneath the trunk of a toppled tree.

The plane turned toward East Pond. The silhouette of Madaket's Eel Point was just visible high on the screen. "This is where the yacht grounded," Terry said, pointing with a finger at a spot along the north shore.

The images lurched and swayed. Howie scanned the multiple lines of rollers, still enormous with hurricane surge. "That's a very high tide," he remarked.

"Much further up on the northern beach than usual. But that'll recede. You'll notice what's missing?"

"The yacht," Howie said.

"Floated off when the tide turned," Terry concluded. "Despite a couple of anchors. I guess Teddy wanted *Shytown* more than we did."

"Your guys are keeping an eye out for it, though?"

"Oh, yeah. I expect we'll recover her. She's likely to be on her way down the Rhode Island coast headed for the Gulf Stream by now. Somebody'll stumble over her."

The plane turned again, southeast toward Whale Island and the cove where Dionis's boat might be. Howie followed the footage intently. There was East Pond, and its narrow outlet to the sound. There was Tuckernuck's grass runway, used on occasion by homeowners with planes. Terry was still talking about *Shytown*, his words buzzing in Howie's ears like horseflies.

"It's a weird spot for it to have grounded anyway," the Coast Guard chief said.

"Why?" Howie asked distractedly. The lagoon had come up on the screen, but disappointingly, the plane's altitude had increased and he couldn't pick out Di's work skiff moored near the dock. Was that because of the rain—too much gray air and water—against the steel-gray metal structure? Or because the boat wasn't there?

Terry sighed at Howie's ignorance. "*Shytown* grounded off the north shore of Tuck. The water is pretty calm there, even in major weather. Really shallow, which is why we can't bring in a Coast Guard boat—but *calm*. I expect people to ground off the *south* shore. Now, those waters are *treacherous*, riddled with currents and sandbars. Makes for great fishing, though. You fish, Howie?"

"Nope," he replied in frustration. "What are you saying, Ter?"

"That I'd bet this grounding was deliberate."

Howie frowned, his attention finally diverted from the screen. "Seriously? Why?"

"It's not like these people were under sail and blown

onto the shoals by hurricane winds. It's a *power* yacht. Only way it could have drifted that far out of the channel is if its engines were cut—or it was deliberately steered into low water."

"Huh," Howie said. "Who decides to ground two million dollars' worth of heroin and then sends up a flare?"

"Somebody who wants to get caught?" Terry suggested.

DIONIS PARKED HER father's truck in the sandy parking area above the boat landing and stared out at what remained of the floating dock.

"Shit," Joe said somberly. "That hurricane wasn't kidding."

The steel gangway had been ripped away and tossed in the middle of the lagoon. The dock it led to had vanished—either under water, or out to sea. Dionis would put money on the latter.

But her skiff was still there. It was riding low and heavy, filled to its oarlocks with seawater—but it was there.

She shoved open her cab door and stepped out into the rain. Lifted her arms and face to it because it was just rain, now, and not her mortal enemy.

"That crazy-ass wind is dropping," Joe said.

He'd noticed the change, too.

Dionis reached back into the cab and pulled out her backpack.

Joe grasped her wrist. "What are you doing?"

"Going home."

Chapter Twenty

"DETECTIVE?"

Merry pulled her rain jacket off as she walked into the police station, showering water around her like an ardent Labrador retriever. Bob Pocock was striding toward her with an expression of such single-minded focus that she was tempted to turn and run. "Yes, sir?"

"Into my office."

Wordlessly, Merry followed him. *He's going to cancel my trip to Paris,* she thought bleakly. *And then I'll have to choose between Peter and my job.* That would be no contest, of course. But she wished it were possible to live two lives at once—the one she'd painstakingly built for herself, and the one she wanted to create with Peter.

The chief hurled himself into his desk chair without inviting her to sit. Merry stood in front of him, feeling raindrops seeping into her shoes.

"I read your report on that boat grounding and drug bust," he said, lifting a printed copy of what appeared to be Merry's emailed synopsis of the *Shytown* crime scene. "Anything to add before you leave town for the next two weeks?"

"I interviewed the female victim's mother, Lorraine Russo."

"And?"

"She has no idea why her daughter was on a luxury yacht filled with heroin."

Pocock snorted contemptuously. "They never do. So, what's your working theory? Murder-suicide, or a falling out between thieves?"

Merry hesitated. Pocock prized intuitive leaps and snap judgments in his detectives. Merry prized objective analysis of the evidence. But in this instance, she had almost none to speak of. She was not about to share Seitz's unverified theory of a wandering gunman. If the speculation turned out to be wrong, Pocock would never let them forget it. She settled for ambivalence. "Either is possible, sir. Unfortunately, we had so little time to gather evidence that there are gaps in what we can know, much less theorize. From an initial study of the wound ballistics, Sergeant Seitz suspects that there may have been two weapons fired at the scene. We'll need confirmation of that from the MBI, of course, and a full autopsy report."

"You only recovered one gun," Pocock countered.

"And the boat, Sergeant Seitz tells me, drifted off its grounding site during the hurricane. The Coast Guard has promised to hunt for it, because of our joint drug recovery, but as you can imagine they have a number of priorities right now. Hurricane damage surveys and rescue ops take precedence."

"Any ID yet on the male victim?"

"Only a tentative one. MBI has not yet responded to our IAFAS print request. But a phone recovered from the scene answers to a number Lorraine Russo—Ashley's mother—says belongs to her daughter's ex-fiancé. I just tested it at the hospital."

"Wait." Pocock looked annoyed. "Put that into plain English."

"Ashley Russo moved to Long Island in April to marry her childhood sweetheart, Kevin Monaghan. However, the two of them recently broke up. Lorraine gave me Monaghan's number so I could interview him about Ashley's life in New York. But Kevin's phone number rings through to the cell phone found on our male victim. I could be wrong, but I am assuming it's Kevin Monaghan in a room at Nantucket Cottage Hospital, masquerading under the false name of Bradley Minot."

Pocock lifted his head and stared at her, transfixed. "Repeat that."

Merry frowned slightly. "I think the male victim we're calling Bradley Minot—the name on his fake ID—is actually Kevin Monaghan. I'd ask him to his face, but he's in a medically induced coma at the moment, with a gunshot wound to his skull."

Pocock said nothing for an instant, as though weighing her words. "What's this joker's prognosis, detective?"

"Better with every hour, I think. Dr. Hughes wants to fly him to Mass Gen as soon as possible. I'm hoping they bring him back to consciousness before he leaves—so that I can interview him first."

"Type up your report," Pocock said with sudden decisiveness, "then get out of here. Concentrate on your wedding. As of now, I'm reassigning this case. Your work is done. Send Seitz in here, will you?"

"When he gets back, sir. He's been liaising at the Coast Guard Station." She should feel relief—she was going to be allowed to fly to Paris Monday after all—but doubt nagged at her. "If I may put in a word for Seitz, sir, he's more than capable of taking over this investigation in my absence."

"Not necessary." Pocock swiveled his chair, turning his back on her. "I'll be handling it myself. Safe travels, detective."

"HANDLING IT *HIMSELF*?" Howie spluttered half an hour later.

Merry had been waiting for him in the parking lot when he returned from Brant Point—sitting behind the wheel of her car, determined to intercept him before Pocock did. She had dutifully filed her report and would be heading back to Cliff Road as soon as she talked to Howie. He'd slid into her passenger seat to talk in private, their shared humidity in the confined space fogging Merry's windshield.

"I know. I thought it was weird, too. His face changed the second I told him the name of the male victim."

"Have you run a background check on Monaghan?"

"Yeah," Merry said. "No red flags. Nothing about his past or profile screams money laundering, drug sales, or luxury yachts. The man's a security guard, Howie. He makes less than we do, if that's possible. I'm beginning to think this was a lover's quarrel—that he got Ashley out on a borrowed boat to romance her back into his arms."

"—Only they shot each other, instead? *Right.*" Howie's tone was dismissive.

"More than half of all murdered women are killed by intimate partners," Merry reminded him. "It's reasonable. We've allowed the heroin to distract us."

"It's a pretty big distraction, you've got to admit. Most

guys don't need two mil worth of drugs to win back their fiancées."

"Maybe he got violent. Pulled the Glock. And Ashley tried to defend herself with her own pistol. She only winged Monaghan, while he got her right in the abdomen."

"Then why wasn't the second gun lying near Ashley?"

"Maybe it was, and Clarence missed it. It was dark on that boat, Howie, and the storm was scaring the hell out of us. Listen—" Merry shifted in her seat to face him. "I can't go back into the station without Pocock blowing up in my face. He made it clear he doesn't want to see me until I'm back from Europe. But *you* have a reason to show up at work. Let me know if the IAFAS report comes back and confirms Monaghan's identity. I'm going to run some searches on my own, at home."

"What are you afraid of, Mer?"

"I don't know." She rubbed at the condensation on the inside of her windshield with her cuff. Almost instantly, the glass clouded again. "I can't accept that Pocock is being *nice* to me. Letting me go home when the island's in chaos and we've got a murder investigation on our hands. Why take over this case himself? Because the victims are from his old hometown of Chicago?"

"You think he's protecting someone? Monaghan, in fact?"

Merry lifted her brows wordlessly.

"It has always seemed weird to me that he left Chicago," Howie said. "Just to run the Nantucket Police. It's not like he even likes this island."

Howie was right; Merry had never understood why a rising star like Pocock, in a major metropolitan department, would throw away his career to bury himself thirty miles out at sea. Unless he wanted to be lost. The force Pocock now ran was a tenth the size of the division he'd previously commanded.

But it could not be possible he was involved in a seaborne heroin ring.

Merry clapped Howie on the shoulder. "Keep your head down. It's possible to overthink."

"I'll see you Saturday." Howie shoved open the passenger door and stepped out of Merry's car.

"Oh, and Seitz—"

He paused.

"I helped Jack Mather file a missing persons report on his daughter today, at the hospital," Merry said. "You're in charge of that case."

A spasm of emotion—relief, anxiety, pain—rippled over Howie's face. "Thanks, Mer," he said. "I *will* find her."

"HOW ARE YOU going to get the boat in, without a dinghy or a dock?" Joe asked.

"Swim." Dionis pulled off her sneakers and sweatshirt and placed them by her backpack. The chill rain immediately raised goosebumps on her arms and neck. Determinedly, she unzipped her jeans. "Pretend I'm wearing a bikini, okay?"

"I can do that."

A ghost of a smile on his face, which was too flushed, and unlike hers, sweating. *Fever*, she thought. *It's not going away, it's getting worse.*

"Let me do it," Joe offered. "I can handle a boat."

"Not with one arm in a sling. And I don't want you

getting your hand in the water," she told him, without adding that it was already infected enough. "Just walk out through the shallows when I bring the skiff in. And bring my backpack and clothes."

He nodded. Dionis slipped on the life vest she'd worn the previous night and, teeth chattering, made her way down the bluff path to the lagoon. Her feet felt raw from her last journey through the same wet sand and dune grass. Cuts in the soles of her feet and along her forearms stung anew. She saw she had a purpling bruise just below her left hip from where she'd slammed into a mooring buoy. Never mind. If everything went right, she'd be in Madaket in an hour.

Joe was coming down the path behind her, her stuff under his left arm. She saw he'd removed the bandage she'd used to bind his right arm to his ribcage; he probably needed it for balance as he negotiated the bluff. She braced herself for the first shock of cold as her feet reached the water, and found, to her surprise, that the ocean felt warmer than the air. Seen in daylight, the storm-surge rollers were less terrifying than they had been at night.

Or maybe they were actually decreasing in strength and size, as the hurricane lost its power.

Eying the skiff and its tethering buoy, Dionis assessed the tide level and current. She thought the sea was bearing south and west—sweeping, again, toward the point of Whale Island and the open water beyond. It was important, she decided, to walk through the shallows further east and north before committing to the waves, so that the current could do most of the work for her, carrying her toward the buoy without a fight.

She reached a place she judged roughly correct for her

gut calculation and sank down into the waves, allowing the life preserver to take her weight. Then she began to knife out with her arms, thrusting hard with her legs in a froglike motion, the mooring buoy rolling crazily in her vision.

For a while, it seemed to come no closer.

Then, when she was starting to tire and feel an immense hopelessness, she was suddenly aware that she was actually moving past it too quickly on the treacherous tide. Panicked that she would miss it, Dionis fought back, kicking out against the roiling lagoon water. She forced herself forward, gasping and desperate, and clutched at the mooring chain with her fingers as it nearly slid by.

She held it with both hands for an instant, breathing deep, then felt her way around the mooring's red sphere to the skiff's painter. Edging her way out along its length, she grasped the prow of the boat, then the gunwale, feeling its sluggish movement beneath her palms—far too much bilge. She steadied herself in the water, legs trailing behind and both hands clenched on the skiff, and hauled herself over the side.

A wave of water sluiced out of the boat as Dionis splashed into its belly. Immediately, she crawled toward a stern locker and pulled it open, fishing in its depths for a bailing bucket. She worked furiously, the exercise warming her chilled body, to empty the skiff of standing water, her spirits slightly diminished each time a rogue wave broke over the side, returning a bucketful for every two she tossed. Roughly ten minutes later, however, she could tell the skiff was riding higher on the sea. Another few minutes of bailing, and Dionis was satisfied.

Taking a deep breath, she untied the skiff's painter and slipped away from the mooring.

Her outboard motor was a carbureted two-stroke, old and edgy. Dionis stripped off the engine's cover and tossed it into the stern locker. Tilted the engine fully down, and squeezed the primer bulb until firm. Then she advanced the throttle in neutral to two-thirds, turned the key (which she'd pinned to her life vest), pushed the choke, and cranked at the same time. Praying the engine would start.

It did.

Jack had always said Dionis was a witch with old motors.

She let out a war whoop of triumph and turned the skiff toward Joe, standing in the shallows beneath the bluff.

HE TOSSED HER clothes and backpack onto the seat amidships as soon as he reached the skiff. Dionis yanked off the life preserver and left it sitting at her feet while she pulled the dry sweatshirt over her chilled body, and worked one wet leg after the other into her stubborn jeans. She shoved her damp, sandy feet into the sneakers, hating the sensation of scour. Joe had taken the helm while she dressed; gathering her wet, black hair into a knot, she crooked a skeptical grin at him.

"Thanks, but forgive me if I can't quite trust a guy whose last outing ended on a sandbar. I'll steer us out of the lagoon and home."

Joe shook his head. "I'm afraid that's not going to work."

"What do you mean?" Dionis's smile faded.

He drew his pistol from his jacket and leveled it at her. "I don't need you anymore, Dionis. And I'm leaving alone."

Chapter Twenty-One

"WHAT ARE YOU doing home so early?" Peter crowed, when Meredith's SUV turned in the Cliff Road drive. "Is it possible we're going to be married at last?"

He set down a wheelbarrow full of broken pieces of peeling white-painted wood and cedar shingles. Merry thrust open her door and reached for him. He smelled of rain and damp leaves and cigar smoke—Hale was across the lawn, and a cigar dangled from the crooked fingers of his left hand. *How Greenwich weathers crisis,* Merry thought. She buried her nose in Peter's chest and breathed deep. His black hair was plastered to his head, soaked beneath a sodden Red Sox cap. His windbreaker was transparent with moisture. She would happily have stayed in his comforting embrace despite the wet that was dousing them, but he shifted and she raised her head.

"Hale and I have been assessing the damage since I got back from the farm a few hours ago."

"And?"

"The attic will need some work. Half the roof walk blew off and the harbor side of the house was thoroughly scoured. Hence the loose shingles we've collected like a dragon's hoard. The back hedge is catawampus."

"A term of art?"

"Take a look at it. You'll agree. There's no other word that quite captures it."

"I've been pulled off the case," Merry said.

His arms tightened around her. "Yay. George managed to make chili for dinner. In a slow cooker. She found most of the ingredients in the pantry, and two pounds of ground beef in the freezer. So, we have many things to celebrate tonight."

"How're the sheep?" Merry asked as he lifted the wheelbarrow and pushed it toward the garage.

"Fine. You should perhaps have asked first about Rafe."

"Oh, I know he's fine, too," she said dismissively. "Rafe and taxes. There's nothing more certain."

"The cranberries, on the other hand . . ."

"You mean, the ones still in the bog?"

"Every single vine is rusted brown from blown salt water. Dead loss."

"I'm sorry," she said.

He parked the barrow inside the garage. "I think I'll just leave all this here until we're back from Europe and have time to take a load to the dump."

"The recycling center."

He quirked a brow. "My, how correct we've become. We'll always have Paris, Merry—and the Nantucket dump. That's what separates us from off-islanders. We remember the *landfill*. Our roots dig deep, girl."

Merry kissed him. "I'm truly sorry about the cranberries. All those months, all that work, all that hope . . ."

Peter shrugged. "Everyone else in New England will be dealing with the same thing. Who knows? Maybe market price will go up. And I've got half a container load to sell!"

THE NURSE NAMED Rebecca glanced up from her computer screen at Nantucket Cottage Hospital and smiled apologetically at the man standing in front of her desk.

"I'm so sorry, Chief Pocock," she said, "but that patient is undergoing treatment right now. I'm not allowed to let you in to see him. Perhaps you could come back tomorrow?"

"I'll wait," Pocock said, and took a seat where he could keep her directly in view.

"MER," HOWIE SAID into her cell phone. "We got the IAFAS report. The guy at Cottage Hospital is definitely Kevin Monaghan, and I agree, he's got nothing like a criminal history. If he went this deep into the drug trade and murder, he did it since moving to New York."

"What's his current health status? Have you talked to the hospital?"

"He's still here," Howie replied. "Summer Hughes says the female victim's body and the evidence you collected are being sent to the lab in Bourne tomorrow. There's such a backlog, we won't get their analysis for weeks or months, however."

"I know," Merry said. "Here's what I've been doing, Seitz—I ran a linked background check on both Robert Pocock and Kevin Monaghan. Also Robert Pocock and Ashley Russo. I even tried Lorraine Russo and Robert Pocock."

"And you turned up nada, right?"

"Absolutely zero. I thought there might be a family relationship, at least, hiding in plain sight, but there's no connection. Is it possible I hate the guy's guts so much, I can't even recognize disinterested kindness when I see it?"

"Bullpucky," Howie said. "The man's never been kind in his life. Particularly to you. I doubt you imagined anything about this, Mer. We'll figure out what's behind it with time."

"Any word on Dionis Mather?"

She felt him shake his head across the distance of the cell phone. Howie sighed heavily. "As soon as I can, I'm going to get the Potts brothers to take me over there, Mer. I don't care if Tuckernuck is not a hurricane priority. She is."

Tim and Phil Potts were police divers on the Nantucket force. Their boat was of low enough draught, Merry suspected, that it might safely dodge the shoals guarding the Tuckernuck Lagoon.

"Hey, it's a police matter now—her dad filed that missing persons report. You'll keep me in the loop?"

"Yeah. Go have some fun."

Fun. Merry glanced over her shoulder. From the sound of voices in the front hallway, her friend Mayling Stern, the Nantucket and New York-based clothing designer, had just arrived for the final fitting of her indescribably beautiful wedding gown. And Merry was still in her work clothes, her hair still damp with rain. Would she ever be able to fake a life of effortless grace and elegance?

"I THOUGHT I should let you know, Howie," Jack Mather said from his bed in Cottage Hospital. "Todd Benson called my cell here, if you can believe, because he couldn't reach Dionis. I told him we'd had no word from her since she went back over to Tuck to feed his horses—and the bastard swore at me. Said if anything had happened to them, he'd sue."

"I hope you send him an outrageous bill," Howie replied. "Di's worth her weight in gold."

"Any sign of her yet?"

"I'm actually in my car," Howie said, "en route to Jackson Point. I hope you don't mind, Jack, but we're going to un-trailer your work skiff and take it over to Tuckernuck. I've got two police divers with me who can pilot the boat."

"The Potts brothers?"

"Yep."

"I've seen them fishing for blues off Tuck's south shore," Jack said. "Tell 'em to swing wide in an S-curve when they thread the lagoon."

"Will do." Howie was relieved that Jack hadn't picked up on the word "divers." He didn't want a man with a heart condition worrying that Di and her boat were at the bottom of the sea. There was no point in saying, either, that anything Jack knew about the shoals guarding Tuckernuck was probably obsolete after the storm surge of the past twenty-four hours. "I'll let you know as soon as we find her."

"MOTHER'S TRYING TO find a flight here on Saturday morning," Georgiana said as she dropped a log on the fire.

"Hope you told her not to knock herself out." Peter's voice was blunt and careless. "Are you actually working over there, Meredith? It's cocktail time."

She looked up from her laptop, which she was running off the generator Tess da Silva had so thoughtfully dispatched from the farm to the Cliff Road house. "I promise I won't even open this thing starting tomorrow morning. I'm just trying to solve a puzzle."

Casey, Georgiana's youngest, looked up from the card table where they had spread out one of the old jigsaws stored in a box for the past few decades, on a shelf with Monopoly and Clue. "You can help me if you want."

"Thanks, sweetheart. I'm planning to sit down over there right after dinner."

"What puzzle?" Peter rose from his comfortable spot on the sofa, winced as his overworked muscles twinged, and came to stand over her. She was sitting in one of the wingchairs at the end of the trestle table where Trey usually worked, catching the fading light of late afternoon. Peter ran his hand softly along her shoulder. She lifted his palm and kissed it.

"Bradley Minot."

"Who?"

"It's not an everyday name, right? I mean, if you were going to fake an ID, wouldn't you go for something a little more John Smith or David Brown? Unless you needed a credit history, too, and a social security number behind it. Which our guy seemed to need."

"Does this have to do with the case you're no longer on?"

"I've been trying to triangulate the victims—Kevin Monaghan and Ashley Russo—with something that looks like criminality. Drugs and guns. Murder-suicide. Or, failing those, with Bob Pocock."

"Your chief?" Peter asked, surprised.

"He went stone cold and lizard-like when I said the name Kevin Monaghan."

"How could you tell? The man makes sharks look cuddly."

"And then he pulled me off this case."

"Because you're getting married?"

"Does that sound like the Pocock you know?"

"He'd be more likely to use the hurricane as an excuse to kill our honeymoon."

"Exactly." Merry snapped her fingers and pointed at Peter in triumph. "It doesn't make sense. So, what's he hiding?"

"Bradley Minot?"

"We found a New York driver's license and credit cards in that name in Kevin Monaghan's wallet. Interesting choice, for a guy who works as a security guard."

"And what happens when you plug Bradley Minot into the internet?" Peter asked, fascinated.

Merry typed the twelve letters into her search bar and hit *Enter*. Immediately, her screen populated with files bearing the name. "Now look what happens when I narrow the search to Chicago," she said, "and hit *Images*."

Peter leaned closer, his eyes narrowed. "What's Pocock doing?"

"Issuing the conclusions of an internal Chicago PD investigation. On Bradley Minot. He was a dirty cop, Peter—killed nearly a year ago in the line of duty."

IT WAS ALMOST five o'clock in the afternoon by the time Howie and the Potts brothers reached Madaket, and the bridge over Hither Creek was still swamped with seawater. They left Howie's car standing in several feet of water on the Madaket Road, and sloshed their way down to Jackson Point.

That took another fourteen minutes.

The Potts brothers, Tim and Phil, were Nantucket natives in their thirties—the sons of a fisherman, in a town that no longer launched a fleet. They had brought their lifelong knowledge of the island's waters, currents, inlets, marshes, kettle ponds, and storms to the Nantucket Police Department, and when they weren't messing around in boats, coordinating with the Coast Guard, they could be found patrolling the summer beaches on department ATVs. They were perpetually bronzed and prematurely weathered. Tim was married and had a three-year-old daughter; Phil, who was four years younger than his brother, had a life partner who was passionate about art quilting and Italian wines. His name was Dylan.

The great thing about the Pottses, Howie decided, was that they were silent and efficient. They had Jack Mather's fiberglass work skiff rolled on its trailer through the standing water at Jackson Point within five minutes, and launched in roughly another two.

He glanced at his watch. Nearly five-thirty, the light failing under the persistent bank of cloud, but the wind had dropped maybe fifty knots since Howie had last stood knee-deep on the boat landing nearly twelve hours before, and the rain was soft enough to be bearable.

"Think we can make it there and back before the day's gone?" he asked Phil.

"We don't have to make it *back*, Seitz," Phil told him. "We just have to make it *out* of the lagoon and through the shoals before dark—and that, my friend, we can do."

Howie was old enough not to hide his own shortcomings. He had too little knowledge of boats and the sea. He let the Pottses handle both and contented himself with sitting in the prow of Jack's boat, watching the dim gray outline of Tuckernuck grow larger on the horizon.

Tim had gotten them fifteen minutes out of Madaket when he wordlessly handed the extended tiller arm to Phil. Howie felt him throttle back the engine as they approached the Lagoon and the precarious underwater sea beds.

"Water's damn high," Tim grunted.

"You mean, the tide's in?" Howie asked.

The other man shook his head. "Storm surge has added four or five feet to the usual depth. Don't think we need to worry about getting caught today. But man—where'd the beach go?"

Howie turned and studied the curving bluff that, along with Whale Island, formed Tuckernuck's Lagoon. He had only been here once before, with Dionis off-season, when the residents wouldn't mind a stranger setting foot on their property. But he thought he remembered a beach. With overturned wood and fiberglass dinghies on it. And other dinghies and boats, moored in the lagoon itself.

Phil whistled. "Christ, Tim—look at that gantry, will you? Guess we're not exactly landing tonight."

The wreckage of the steel access ramp to the floating dock was half submerged, the dock itself missing. But Howie was distracted by everything else he couldn't see.

"Di's boat," he said. "It's not here."

"Hell, neither are the local dinghies," Phil pointed out. "Neither is the dock. I bet everything tore off and floated away last night."

"There's a truck parked up on the bluff," Tim offered. "Recognize it, Seitz?"

Howie squinted. It looked like something Jack Mather

would drive around Tuck's unpaved roads—old, low maintenance, dependable. And it was the only vehicle visible from the lagoon. Jack and Di probably used it to shuttle luggage and clients to the beach before the hurricane hit.

But if she'd come back yesterday afternoon—if she'd *actually reached Tuckernuck*—wouldn't Dionis have driven that truck straight to Northern Light and checked on the horses?

Howie felt his stomach pitch with misery. "Jesus, guys," he said. "This isn't looking good."

Phil was weaving his way gingerly through the narrow entrance to the Lagoon, his eyes darting between the horizon and the bottom. The water was opaque and sullen after the storm; it gave up no secrets.

"What am I going to tell Jack?" Howie muttered bitterly.

A red buoy was in sight. Phil cut the engine. Tim was moving toward Howie in a crouch, a boat hook in his hand. As Howie edged aside, Tim leaned forward and with a single deft movement picked up a mooring line and ran the skiff's painter through it.

I've got to get better at boats, Howie thought irrelevantly, *if I want Di in my life.*

Di. *Life.*

He felt sick to his stomach. She was gone. And he hadn't told her he loved her, at Lola's all those hours ago. He would never get the chance—

Phil Potts clapped him on the shoulder. "Tim and I'll throw on our wetsuits and get into shore. Take a look at the truck," he said. "Maybe she left the keys under the back wheel."

Bob Pocock studied the insensate figure of the man who was definitely *not* Bradley Minot as the duty nurse, a short, barrel-chested guy with the rolling gait of a wrestler, deftly changed the sheets without disturbing his patient.

"You find out who shot him?" the nurse asked.

Pocock's eyelids flickered. "Not yet."

"What happens when we fly him out to Mass Gen? Does the Boston PD take over?"

"No." Pocock met the nurse's friendly gaze, his own expressionless. *Wayne,* read the nurse's name tag. "Are you planning to transfer him to Boston soon, Wayne?"

"I don't know. The docs make that decision."

The police chief absorbed this in silence.

Wayne gathered the soiled sheets into his arms and rolled toward the door.

"Has he said anything?" Pocock asked suddenly.

Wayne shook his head, lips compressed. "Not yet. Too far under."

"Good," Pocock breathed to himself.

Chapter Twenty-Two

WHEN MEREDITH AWOKE Friday morning, she was alone in the bed. Peter was an early riser—the habit of a farmer—and from the faint scent of coffee she could smell on the air, he'd been up for some time. She lay still, eyeing the gray light that filtered through the window shades. Brant Point Coast Guard Station's foghorn muttered repetitively in the background, but it was a sound Merry had known from birth and she found it soothing. She almost punched her pillow and slipped back into a dream, but an indefinable difference in the atmosphere teased her muddled consciousness. Then she realized what it was.

The rain had stopped.

She slipped from beneath the comforter and raised the nearest blind.

No sun yet—that was too much to ask—but the clarity of the light displayed every last blade of grass freshly washed and distinct under the clouded sky. A light breeze lifted the blue-violet heads of hydrangea flowers, no longer sodden and bowed, above the bushes lining the crushed shell drive. Merry's pulse quickened. Nantucket was still a storm-tossed disaster area and the island's cleanup would take weeks—but she was getting married tomorrow, and the omens were favorable.

She clawed at the window's stubborn, ancient frame, swollen fat with moisture, and succeeded in raising the sash. She leaned out and took a deep breath. The air's grace notes were rain and green, salt, something spicy off the moors, and a mix of all the flowers still open to the world. Merry closed her eyes, her heart singing. It was the deepest smell in the world—the smell of *home*.

Peter rapped lightly on the half-open door behind her.

"Coffee," he said.

She took the mug, made as she liked it—with steamed milk poured in first—and sighed after the first sip.

"When are we on today?" he asked her.

"Not until four. When we dress for the rehearsal. Or rather—for the dinner afterward."

"Got it. Feel like getting on your bike?"

"I'd love to," she said. "Maybe around noon. Right now . . . I've got a few last errands to run."

JOHN FOLGER HAD a rake in his hands when Merry pulled up to Tattle Court. He was dressed comfortably in a plaid flannel shirt and a pair of worn jeans, a baseball cap on his charcoal-gray hair. There was a boat trailer parked inexplicably on the front lawn, with John's prized toy—his fishing boat—lashed down against the hurricane with far more ropes than necessary. Her grandmother Sylvie would never have tolerated wheel-marks in the grass, but since Merry's departure from the family home a few years before, the two Folger men had abandoned the slightest pretense of caring about other people's opinions. They lived happily in a male preserve.

"Meredith! You survived the gale!"

"How was the storm cellar, Dad?"

"Cozy. Ralph brought down some shag carpet this year. We played a lot of poker. I took thirteen dollars off your grandfather." He propped the rake against the front porch railing. "Want some coffee?"

"No, thanks. Is Ralph around?"

"Down at the Wharf Rats. Place sustained a bit of damage. Aren't you supposed to be having your hair done or something?"

"Tomorrow," she said. "Dad, I stopped by to ask you a question."

"All right. Come in."

Merry followed him into the kitchen, which was cluttered with an extraordinary collection of old magazines, tools, exuberant house plants and fishing equipment. She lifted Toby the cat off the kitchen table and sat down with him in her lap. John poured himself coffee and offered Merry cranberry nut bread. "Ralph bakes when it's raining."

"I know." She took a slice. "Peter's harvest is shot to hell."

"Not surprised. But he's not dependent on cranberries for a living. Happily, neither are you."

"True. Dad, would you or Ralph be devastated if I quit my job?"

Her father drank his coffee deliberately. "Is that why you're here? Hell, Ralph and I have had a running bet ever since you got engaged. He says you'll stay on. I've got fifty bucks on you throwing in the towel."

Merry felt a flare of indignation. "You backed a quitter?"

He quirked a brow. "I don't know. Did I?"

"This isn't because of the wedding," she attempted. "Or Peter. He knows how important my work is to me—I wouldn't have agreed to marry him otherwise."

"School, then? You want to go back?"

She assessed him dubiously. "I never told you that."

"I know you're afraid you never got a thorough education. More of a technical degree. I've been a little worried that with Peter, you feel . . ."

"Outmatched? Yeah, there's some of that." Merry wiped her fingers on a paper napkin plucked from the holder in the middle of the kitchen table. Ralph's quick breads were deliciously buttery. "I'm seduced by the idea of certain things, I won't lie. Like not having to work for a living. Like having oceans of found time, when I can read and learn to cook and get into better physical shape and . . ."

"See the world," John suggested.

"Yes!"

"Have children, even. Raise them yourself."

"Quite possibly."

"So, what's keeping you? You've put in a lot of years, Meredith. Paid your dues. I think you've earned the right to kick back."

She took a deep breath. "I love what I do. I love this island. Love knowing that it's partly my job to keep it safe."

Her father waggled his head from side to side, then finished his coffee. "That's a family failing. Not going to argue with you."

"Here's the thing." Merry set Toby on the floor and dusted cat hair off her hands. "I think it's possible I'll be fired this morning. And I wanted to talk to you about it first."

"Fired? *Why?*" John Folger frowned at her.

"For accusing my chief of being an accessory to murder."

JACK MATHER WAS sitting on the edge of his bed, fully dressed, when Howie tapped on the door of his hospital room.

"Going somewhere, sir?"

Jack smiled. "Home, I guess. Only takes twenty-four hours to recover from a stent, but they kept me here longer because of the hurricane."

Howie frowned. "You're not driving yourself, are you?"

"Can't," Jack admitted. "Di took the truck. You saw it out in Madaket, didn't you?"

Howie nodded. "Can I give you a lift?"

"Nah, I can tell by the uniform you're on duty." Jack shrugged, his gaze sliding away. "I asked the nurse to call a taxi. I'll be fine."

"I don't think you should be alone, sir."

"I take it you didn't find my girl." Jack's hands clenched on the mattress edge.

"Not yet." Howie had come to Cottage Hospital to break exactly this news. That Dionis's boat was nowhere to be found between Madaket and Tuckernuck. That Jack's truck was locked and parked above the lagoon. That it looked as though his precious daughter had seen to the Benson horses, returned to the dock, then tried to make it back home before the hurricane completely hit. And had foundered in gale-force swells.

That Howie was conducting a search for a body, now.

But Howie said none of this. He clung stubbornly to a sliver of hope. It had been growing too dark last night for him or the Pottses to walk to Northern Light and back without risking a grounding on the shoals as they attempted to leave Tuck. They hadn't been able to confirm that Dionis had been to the barn.

Jack forced himself upright and swayed uncertainly. Howie went to his side and grasped his elbow. "Should I call for a wheelchair?"

"Just walk with me," he said. "I can make it to the door."

They had almost made it there when Summer Hughes walked briskly toward them from an adjoining corridor.

"Sergeant Seitz," she said. "Your patient is awake. Would you let Meredith Folger know?"

THE EIGHTY-THREE-FOOT GROUNDFISHING dragger, *Maisy B.*, put out from Leonard's Wharf and the Port of New Bedford before dawn that morning. Her four-man crew had fretted through the enforced inactivity of Hurricane Teddy for most of the previous week. Commercial fishermen who work the shallows of the Nantucket Shoals—*Maisy*'s preferred ground, seven miles east of Siasconset—stay out of port for at least ten days, and *Maisy*'s captain, Josh Orsona, had no intention of getting caught away from port as the hurricane approached. He'd kept his crew idle in New Bedford, buying beer and playing cards at Club Madeirense.

The boot-shaped shoal known as Rose and Crown, which sat about ten miles southeast of Nantucket, was just coming up at port and Great Rip to starboard when Orsona, at his vessel's helm, narrowed his eyes. "Hey, Jimmy," he called over his shoulder. "Your eyes are better than mine. What's that look like, dead ahead?"

His first mate joined him in *Maisy*'s wheelhouse, staring over the forward net drums at an indistinct object on the horizon. Then his eyes strayed to the smaller of the dragger's radar screens. "Looks like a dinghy from here," he said. "Maybe a storm drift? Good thing you saw that before you were dead on top of it."

Jimmy was right; the net drums partially blocked the view over the bow. "Get out on the port bow," Josh told him, "and I'll pull alongside. You see if it's worth towing."

Three minutes later the dragger had caught up with the drifting vessel and slowed its engine speed to a dead crawl. *Not* a dinghy, Josh saw now, but a fiberglass skiff with an outboard engine still lowered in the water, cut dead and silent. Jimmy, crouched in the bow, tensed suddenly and shouted.

"Ahoy! Ahoy! You need help?"

He peered over the side another instant, then shoved himself to his feet and sped back to the wheelhouse.

"There's a guy lying on the floor of the skiff, Cap'n," he said urgently, "and he's not answering."

The skiff had slipped to stern by this time. Josh glanced over his shoulder and saw it bobbing in *Maisy*'s wake. "I'll come about," he said. "Get Cody up here."

As he began to turn his boat around, his red-haired son materialized at his elbow. Cody was nineteen, four months out of New Bedford High School, and it was his job to ready the refrigerated fish lockers down below.

"Yeah, Dad?" he said.

"I need you to take a swim."

Cody didn't argue, just pulled his sweatshirt over his head.

"Get a painter from Jimmy, dive in, and tie it to the bow cleat of that skiff coming up to starboard."

"Okay." Cody left the wheelhouse. He was a kid of few words.

Josh cut his engine. An instant later, he saw a splash

go up off *Maisy*'s side, and caught a glimpse of his son crawling steadily through the water. The sea depth over the Nantucket Shoals averaged a fathom and a half, not much deeper than a swimming pool, and Cody managed the distance easily. He grasped the skiff's gunwale with one arm and cleated the painter with his free hand. Then he waved to the wheelhouse and began to swim back to *Maisy B.*

Jimmy helped Cody back on board, then began to haul in the painter. The skiff came alongside, and Jimmy cleated it there before jumping into the belly of the other boat.

He lifted the inert form over his shoulder in a fireman's carry. Cody and the last of the four crewmen—one of Josh's veterans, Teague Plager—reached forward to grasp the man's legs. *Unconscious*, Josh thought as he watched them sling the body aboard, *or dead.*

He reached for his VHF radio. Either way, the Coast Guard needed to know.

Chapter Twenty-Three

MERRY SAT IN her car near Tattle Court for a few seconds after saying goodbye to her father. She was thinking about the pieces of her puzzle that failed to connect to anything, the pieces that were still missing, and the ones she needed to turn over in her mind until they dovetailed with the map she was slowly constructing. Then she pulled out her cell phone and dialed a number in Chicago.

If Lorraine Russo hadn't picked up on the fourth ring, Merry might have stifled her impulse to talk to the woman again, and the day would have turned out differently. But Lorraine answered. And Merry asked her the question that had been lurking in her mind ever since her digital search the previous evening.

"Did your daughter Ashley know a man named Brad Minot?"

"Brad? Of course. He was Kevin's best friend, you know, from the time they were little boys. They did Scouts together, were on the same Little League team. It was terrible when Brad was killed. Kevin sort of lost a brother. And then learning he'd been taking bribes from gangs—the whole community was shocked."

"And Ashley?"

Lorraine hesitated. "She took the whole thing pretty hard. I think she'd always had a soft spot for Brad. Maybe a crush, even. But it was after he was killed last fall, and the scandal came out, that Ash and Kevin really got together—as though they had both learned what mattered, and weren't going to waste any more time." Lorraine paused. "Why are you interested in Brad, detective?"

"I'm trying to understand your daughter's mindset over the past few months, ma'am," Merry offered vaguely. "That may shed some light on her death. Did Kevin take the police investigation badly, as well?"

"Oh, yes—that's why he moved away from Chicago. He said he didn't believe in justice anymore."

Merry's pulse quickened. "Why is that?"

"He never believed that Bradley had done anything wrong. Said it was a mistake, and that the truth would never come out unless the police tracked down Brad's killer. Which they don't seem likely to do. I mean, these gangs . . ."

Lorraine's voice trailed away. The facelessness of organized urban crime was useful, Merry thought, if you were attempting to misdirect an investigation. All that was really known about the gang that allegedly shot Bradley Minot, for instance, was that it was an Asian-run syndicate, importers and distributors of fentanyl and heroin, whose kingpins had mostly evaded arrest. Any number of atrocities could be laid at their door, both actual and fictional.

"It seems so strange," Lorraine persisted, "that Ashley should be gone, now, too—shot, like Brad. Kevin must feel that he's cursed."

Or the people he loves, Merry thought. "Would you say he was bitter about Brad Minot's death?"

"Very," Lorraine agreed. "I think that's why Ashley was so important in his life. She was so caring, detective—such a loving person—that she helped Kevin get through his grief. Ashley decided to move East because she thought he needed her. She never turned her back on someone. That's why I was surprised when she suddenly broke up with Kevin a few months ago. It wasn't like her to drop a friend."

"Did she ever explain her decision, Mrs. Russo?"

"Not really. I got the feeling Kevin had hurt her somehow. I was hoping it would blow over and they'd get back together."

"When you say hurt," Merry attempted, "did he lash out at Ashley? Or become physically violent?"

"Oh, I'm sure he never *hit* her, if that's what you're asking," Lorraine protested hurriedly. "Kevin was a perfect gentleman. He was an altar boy at St. Michael the Archangel, you know, years ago. Even if the wedding was off, I'm sure he and Ash were still good friends."

The kind who go on a luxury cruise together, Merry thought.

"Did either of them ever mention a man named Robert Pocock? Or one named Matthew Rinehart?"

"You asked me about a Matt before," Lorraine pointed out. She was starting to tire of the questions, Merry sensed, her grief overcoming her desire to be helpful. "And no, I don't recall Ashley saying she knew anyone by that name. Pocock doesn't ring a bell either. Are you saying they were friends of hers?"

"Friends of Brad Minot's," Merry said. "Rinehart was his partner."

"That's right," Lorraine said thoughtfully. "A Matt Rinehart was wounded, wasn't he? In the shootout that killed Brad? I'm sure Ash never knew him, but Kevin may have. You've talked to Kev, right?"

"That's been a bit difficult. I'm afraid we haven't connected yet."

"Of course—you've had a *hurricane,* haven't you? I've been so distracted with all that's happened, I haven't really been following much." Lorraine drew breath on a sob. "I keep thinking this is some sort of nightmare, detective, and I'll wake up to find Ashley's right here."

"I'm so sorry, Mrs. Russo, for all you've lost."

"You'll call me when you have news?"

"Absolutely," Merry said.

Whether Bob Pocock liked it or not.

TERRY SAMSON REACHED Howie Seitz at Marine Home, where he was buying a tarpaulin to rig over his damaged bedroom window. It would be days before shipments of plywood arrived by ferry, and weeks before Howie would be able to find a handyman capable of replacing both window frame and glass. In the meantime, he'd emailed the off-islanders who owned his caretaker apartment and told them about the damage. They had filed an insurance claim, and Howie had deployed electric fans throughout the space to hasten the drying process.

His heart quickened when he heard the master boatswain's voice, then thudded painfully as dread replaced hope. "Hey, Terry. Got anything for me?"

"We found your girl's boat."

Howie's fingers spasmed on his phone.

"It was drifting, out of gas, off Nantucket Shoals."

Terry hesitated. "There's no easy way to say this, Howie—Dionis Mather wasn't in it. Just a guy with a raging fever and a gunshot wound in his hand. If you want to question him, we just brought him in to Cottage Hospital."

Howie ended his call and stood motionless for an instant in the crowded aisle, as islanders slid past him, searching for repair supplies for their damaged homes. He'd been taken off the *Shytown* case. Pocock was handling it now. But *Shytown* had just run dead into Dionis Mather, and he wasn't about to let this go.

He dialed Merry Folger's cell. She picked up immediately.

"Detective. You dressed, or officially on vacation?"

"I'm on my way to the station," she told him. "Not that I'm supposed to be. I'm supposed to be drinking champagne. What's up, Seitz?"

"Kevin Monaghan is awake," he said, "and our second shooter is in the ER."

THE MAN WHOM Josh Orsona and the *Maisy B.* had saved was conscious and sitting up in his bed, sipping from a plastic cup, when Merry and Howie Seitz tapped on his open door.

"Severely dehydrated," Suzie the ER nurse had told them, "and feverish from an infected gunshot wound in his left palm. He's getting intravenous antibiotics right now along with systemic pain meds. He'll need surgery with an orthopedic hand specialist on the mainland as soon as possible—several of the small bones in his hand are completely shattered—but that's a problem for another day."

"Has he told you anything about himself?"

"Just his name—Joe Williams. We'll get his address one of these days." Suzie, whose ER was showing the strain of patients reporting with minor injuries in the aftermath of the hurricane, looked justifiably harassed.

Joe Williams. *Now that*, Merry thought, *is a perfectly bland alias. Bradley Minot was a far more calculated one.*

"Mr. Williams?" she asked from the doorway, Howie looming behind her.

The dark-haired man glanced over at her. Roughly mid-thirties, she guessed, and handsome in an obvious way. He flashed a grin, as though taking his ease in a beach club deck chair. But she detected wariness in his blue eyes.

Merry flipped open her badge and held it aloft. "Nantucket Police. We'd like to ask you a few questions."

"I'm sure you would." Joe Williams held out his right hand. His left was neatly bandaged and lying at his side, the IV feeding into his arm. "May I see that, please?"

Merry handed him her badge without a word. Seitz fished his out of his pocket and dropped it on the mattress. Williams made a show of examining them both. "A detective and a sergeant. What am I supposed to have done?"

"Stolen a boat," Seitz suggested. "At the very least. The skiff you were found in belongs to a Nantucket resident named Jack Mather. It was last used by his daughter, Dionis."

"Never heard of her," Joe said, and set down their badges.

"Grab a chair, Seitz," Merry suggested, and sat in one herself. She drew a notebook and pen from her shoulder bag.

"I'd rather stand." Howie's gaze was hard and angry; he looked like he might take a swing at the patient if he continued to sidestep their questions. "Where'd you find Dionis Mather's skiff?"

"It floated by me," Joe replied, "and being desperate, I climbed in. So, shoot me."

"Somebody else has already done that," Merry observed.

Howie's fingers flexed warningly. "What have you done with Di?"

"Who?" Joe frowned in puzzlement.

"The girl who owns the skiff, you asshole!"

He shrugged. "I just jumped in an empty boat."

Merry tossed a quelling glance at Howie. "Care to tell us how it happened?"

"I was in distress off Hyannis a few days ago as the storm rolled in—I shouldn't have been out on the water, but I'm not much of a sailor and didn't know any better," Joe said sheepishly. "My sail ripped away in a wind gust, and I had no motor. I panicked, I admit—and then I injured myself. With a flare gun."

He lifted his bandaged hand. "That skiff passed within twenty yards of me, and it had an outboard motor. I weighed the odds—no working engine on my sailboat, versus obviously unmoored powerboat, complete with engine—and abandoned ship. I swam out to the skiff and managed to pull myself on board with my good hand. Problem was, the skiff's outboard was out of gas."

"But the boat had a VHF radio," Howie pointed out. "Did you send an SOS to the Coast Guard?"

This, of course, could be verified. Merry watched Joe hesitate as he calculated whether they already knew the answer to this question.

"I'm afraid I wasn't thinking very clearly." He rubbed his forehead with his good hand. "Pain, probably. And then, when the hurricane hit, I just lay flat in the bottom of the boat and held on. *God*, that was a nightmare. I should have capsized. I should have drowned. It's a miracle I survived. But by the time the storm passed—I was delirious. I don't remember much after that. Until I came to, on board the Coast Guard boat."

There was a pause, as the three people in the room surveyed one another. Merry caught the faintest suggestion of relief suffusing Joe's face, and it made her angry in a way she did not like to feel on the day before her wedding.

Because Ashley Russo would never be getting married to anyone, now. And that was the fault of the man lying in front of her.

"You survived," Merry agreed. "So did Kevin Monaghan, Joe. He told us all about the last few minutes on *Shytown* Wednesday night. How he'd collected photographic and audio evidence against you for months. How he wanted the Coast Guard to catch you red-handed with a shipment of heroin, so he deliberately grounded the yacht off Tuckernuck and fired a distress rocket. He's in a room down the hall, actually, recovering from a head wound delivered by a .38 Special round. That's an old-fashioned bullet, low velocity, fired from a gun most cops don't use anymore. I'm thinking you got that wound in your palm when you took the Smith & Wesson out of Kevin Monaghan's grasp. And shot him with it."

Joe stared from Meredith to Howie incredulously. "What are you talking about?"

"*Your gun was found*," she said. "In the bottom of

Dionis Mather's skiff. The Coast Guard impounded it as evidence this morning. You were probably too delirious to notice, Joe . . . or should I call you Matthew Rinehart?"

For a fraction of a second, he didn't move. Then he lurched out of bed as though he could run away from the two of them. The IV line hampered him. Its stainless steel stand rolled and toppled as he tugged his way to the door. Seitz stepped forward and grasped Matt Rinehart's bandaged hand, hard. He swore in pain, and Seitz twisted the left arm behind Rinehart's back.

"Matthew Rinehart, I am arresting you for the murder of Ashley Russo," Merry said. "You have the right to remain silent."

Chapter Twenty-Four

"DETECTIVE," BOB POCOCK said, as Merry slid out of her police SUV at a few minutes past eleven that Friday morning, and walked deliberately across the parking lot toward him. "I thought I told you to stay home. Or is the wedding canceled?"

"I'm surprised you're not at Cottage Hospital. Everyone else seems to be." Merry stopped short next to the chief. He was locking his car.

He turned without a word and began walking toward the station.

"Kevin Monaghan woke up," Merry called after him. "Don't you think you should tell me the truth about Brad Minot before he does?"

Pocock came to a halt in the middle of the parking lot. Stood still for the space of three seconds. Merry counted. Then he said, "My office. Detective." And walked on.

Merry followed. It helped to know that Seitz was driving into the police lot right behind her.

A few heads swiveled in surprise as she walked through the station's desk area, past the conference room and interview rooms, down the hallway to the chief's office. Merry avoided eye contact and thus all questions or

conversation. Pocock had left the door open. She closed
it behind her.

"Have something to get off your chest, detective?" he
said.

From anyone else, the words might have carried a
sexual innuendo. Not Pocock. His soul was too arid for
subtext.

"Bradley Minot. A thirty-year-old officer who'd logged
eight years with the Chicago police." Merry said, "He was
killed in the line of duty two years ago, shot in the head
during a drug bust on the North Side. His partner, Matthew Rinehart, was wounded in the leg but able to call
for backup."

"So even in a backwater like this, you know how to
pull up old news online." Pocock, Merry noticed, had
abandoned his usual avoidance and was looking directly
at her. On another day that might have been unnerving.
Today, she welcomed the challenge. It meant she wasn't
wrong.

"Minot has gone down as a dirty cop," she said. "On
the take from the same gang that eventually killed him.
Evidence at the scene and an internal investigation—by
the division you headed, sir—concluded that Minot was
deliberately set up and taken out by his criminal buddies.
A police source reported Minot wasn't happy just taking bribes to look the other way—he got ambitious. He
wanted a share of the gang's profits. They got rid of him
and moved on."

Pocock's hands were still, his laptop closed. "Why
are you raking all this up, detective? It's out of your
jurisdiction."

"But you're not," Merry said softly. "Did you know

Officer Minot, sir? When you were deputy chief of the Special Investigative Group of the Bureau of Detectives with the Chicago Police?"

"I knew his name," Pocock replied, almost unwillingly.

"I wondered," Merry persisted, "because I found a picture of you—online, again—delivering the internal investigation's report. It tied up the tragic story neatly and allowed senior officers to pledge greater oversight of police corruption. You had to resign, of course—fall on your sword—take responsibility for the lapse in the ranks. Take a minor post instead, halfway across the country from Chicago, in what you like to call a *backwater*. You were given good enough recommendations from your superiors that the town selectmen never probed deeper than your resume."

She waited. It was questionable at this point whether Pocock was still breathing. But eventually his nostrils flared and he said, "What's your point, detective?"

"Somebody else quit, too. Officer Matthew Rinehart— the guy who was shot in the leg during the firefight that killed his partner, Brad Minot. Rinehart earned a commendation for bravery. I bet he has nightmares, though. Post-traumatic stress. I know I would, if I had tried and failed to save a partner's life—Seitz, for instance. I'd see his face in front of my eyes for the rest of my life. And I'd never come to terms with failing him."

Merry paused. Pocock was studying her impassively. He was unlikely to help her out, offer the facts so they could both go home. She glanced at her watch; she'd promised Peter she'd be back by noon for a bike ride. And suddenly she was impatient with all the bullshit. For the first time in their mutual history, Merry gave up standing before the chief's desk. She reached for one of the old chairs she'd ordered for the office when her father was still chief, and sank into it.

"I mentioned that to Matt Rinehart when I talked to him at the hospital a few minutes ago," she said. "And he laughed, chief. Right in my face, right in front of Seitz. He doesn't give a rat's ass for the memory of Brad Minot. Because he killed him, didn't he? And you helped cover it up."

"Matthew's here? In the hospital?" Pocock stuttered. "Is he hurt?"

"He'll live." Merry's brows drew down. "Why'd you protect him? A dirty cop with all his fingers in the drug business?"

Pocock looked away, through the sole window that lit his office, at a maple tree whose leaves, just beginning to turn red, had been completely stripped from its branches by hurricane-force winds. "I thought he deserved a second chance."

"Why?"

Pocock shook his head once, as though clearing it of cobwebs. "Because he's my stepson."

Merry said nothing for an instant. She had suspected some sort of relationship, but the surnames were different and Pocock had no wife she'd ever heard of. More dead history not worth sharing. But she observed, "Brad Minot was someone's son, too."

"He was dead anyway." Pocock looked at her then. "I couldn't be *sure* Matt set him up and killed him. It was possible the evidence linking Minot to the drug ring was authentic. *Not* planted. Not something Matt had used to deflect attention when Brad got too close to the truth."

"You're telling me what you wanted to believe."

"What I convinced myself of—yes." Pocock's gaze went out the window again. "I told Matt he had to resign. That we both did. Leave Chicago. I thought he'd take the chance to live a different life."

Like you? Merry thought, recalling every moment Pocock had resisted getting to know the Nantucket community, the landscape of the island, the rhythm of days by the sea.

"There are some people, detective, who find it impossible to change. Even when their lives depend on it. Matt is one of those. Has he confessed?"

"No." Merry rose from her seat. "But we found two guns. He handled both. The Glock he owned for protection, and the old-fashioned, low velocity Smith & Wesson Kevin Monaghan used as a security guard. Rinehart fired the Glock into Ashley Russo's stomach and turned the Smith & Wesson on Monaghan. The wound and missile ballistics will damn him."

Pocock nodded and heaved a deep sigh.

"We cuffed Rinehart to his bed," Merry said, turning at the door. "The hospital will release him to a cell here later today. Oh, and chief? I can't work for a man I can't trust. I'll leave as soon as I type my letter of resignation. Call it my wedding gift to you."

CAITLYN MARSHALL, ON duty at the Nantucket Police Department's reception desk, took the call from New York a few minutes later. She tried to route it to Scott Tredlow, the department's emergency management coordinator, but he was out at Surfside responding to a report of systematic looting among the unoccupied beach houses damaged from hurricane surf, and the call went to voicemail.

Two seconds later, her phone rang again.

"What do you not understand about the sentence *I demand to speak to an officer right now?*" the caller said. "Don't give me voicemail. Hell, give me the police chief!"

Caitlyn quailed. She was never, never, never to send a call straight to Pocock without verifying his availability first. But she had seen Meredith Folger enter his office and shut the door.

She thought quickly.

Howie Seitz knew something about Tuckernuck Island. And blessedly, he had just walked through the station door.

"Take this," she said urgently, handing him the phone. "The guy's nuts."

He lifted his brows in surprise. "Send it to my desk."

"One moment, sir," Caitlyn told the caller. "Sergeant Seitz will be taking your report."

She exhaled in relief and went back to eating her Scotch-Irish cake.

Howie picked up on the first ring. "Seitz," he said.

"Todd Benson, officer. I'm calling to report a break-in at my home on Tuckernuck Island."

Howie choked on a sip of coffee. Images cascaded through his mind—Benson delivering a perfect spiral in last year's Super Bowl game, his chiseled features unsmiling for the press, Benson on the cover of *The New York Times Magazine* with that same million-dollar arm thrown casually over the tanned shoulder of his wife.

And then, Dionis's face: scintillating in Howie's mind as though outlined in neon.

"Where are you calling from, sir?" Howie said.

"New York. I've got video footage of the break-in from security cameras at the house. It came over the monitor a few minutes ago."

"Can you describe what it shows, sir?"

"A woman. Standing right there in the foyer. She must have come through the front door. My security people got a breaking-glass alarm first, then a motion detector signal, then the footage. It's pretty brazen, and pretty unequivocal. She looks straight at the camera, like she *wants* to be identified."

Howie's heart began to sing. "Send me the footage via email," he suggested.

A few seconds later, he hit *play*.

"I SHOULD JUST shoot you," Joe had said to her as he'd leveled the gun the day before, "but I'm feeling kind. So, get out of the boat as fast as you can, Dionis, before I change my mind."

She had stared at him in disbelief, all her doubts about the stranger who'd walked in from the storm rising sickly in her throat. "Are you crazy?"

The gun exploded, and Dionis fell sideways, clutching her seat with shaking hands. "Jesus!"

"Get out of the boat."

Half-crouching, she rolled over the side, her breath tearing through her chest in panicked gasps, lagoon water above her knees. "You're a fucking asshole, Joe!"

The gun fired again. A bullet hopscotched through the waves. *He was shooting at her.*

Bent double, Dionis darted toward shore, her arms flailing.

She turned to look when she reached the bluff, just in time to see her skiff wheel in a semicircle. Joe's back faced her and his gaze fixed on the opening in the lagoon, where the channel wove through the shifting shoals, to deeper water beyond.

But instead of heading west for Madaket, he turned toward Whale Point, at the south end of the lagoon.

He's going to ground the skiff, Dionis thought frantically, craning her neck to follow his course. The sandbars off that south shore were good only for gray seal haul-outs and shipwrecks. She waited for the shift in octave that would signal an engine churning through too-shallow water, but it never came.

The storm surge must be lifting her boat over shoals that normally would have doomed it.

Joe had lied from the moment he'd walked into the barn. *Nothing he told me was true.* And like an idiot, she had *helped* him. Dionis let out a guttural shriek of frustration and rage, then forced herself up the bluff to the relative warmth of her truck.

But a fresh insult awaited her there.

In her desperate rush to get out of Joe's pistol range, she had left her backpack behind in the skiff. Her keys were in it.

So, of course, was her cell phone.

During the hour it took her to walk back to Northern Light, Dionis decided what she had to do.

Todd Benson was certain to have installed a state-of-the-art security system in his trophy home, laughable as that would seem to the majority of Tuckernuck's residents. There were rumors of deer hunters landing on the island in the autumn after everyone had gone, and helping themselves to canned goods and beer from the pantries of unsecured houses. Benson wouldn't like that. He'd want to protect his wine cellar and his weight room. His security system would have digital video cameras, and the feed would be monitored twenty-four/seven. All Dionis had to do was smash a window, stand in front of a camera, and wave for help.

Then she'd take a hot bath and raid Benson's pantry for lunch—because Mandy's barn cupboards were now completely bare. She hoped the Bensons weren't depressingly vegan. But either way, a helicopter was sure to land in the front yard within hours.

Dionis turned Afterglow and Honeybear out into the paddock and made sure their feeder had enough hay. She left the sliding barn door wide open to the fresh poststorm air, and turned her face up to the gray sky, relieved to find the rain had ended. Then she picked up a pitchfork and set off up the drive to the main house.

It was a shingle-style palace of a kind that was commonplace on Nantucket, but utterly unusual on Tuckernuck Island. The architect had minimized the impression of size by thrusting a modest central building, with a deeply shaded wraparound porch, to the foreground, as though it were the original old house further generations had expanded. Dionis peered up at the summit of the pitched roof, where a lantern—a glass-enclosed cupola—echoed those on older island houses. Flanking the house's central mass on either side were single-story wings that fell back toward the ocean. Dionis suspected that a rear deck or terrace connected all three elements of the house, and that the back of Benson's home opened fully to views of sea and sky.

But she didn't bother to check if her assumption was correct. She knew a bit about security systems—they focused on doors and windows, as well as the sound of breaking glass and motion detection. She might as well attack her problem right at the front door.

This was solid and painted hydrangea blue, one of the Nantucket Historical Commission's approved paint colors; but surrounding the sides and top of the door were divided glass lights, another traditional detail borrowed from centuries of Federal architecture. Dionis hefted her pitchfork by its tines, and swung the wooden pole handle with her best knock-it-out-of-the-park baseball swing. Three of the panes shattered bewitchingly. And a horn blared, followed by a siren.

"Whoa, Nelly!" Dionis blurted out, startled by the sudden cacophony. She dropped the pitchfork, wrapped the sleeve of her sweatshirt over her hand, and punched the remaining shards of glass from the window frame. Then she reached inside and fumbled until she found the deadbolt.

She stood a moment in the open doorway, absorbing the gorgeous satin expanse of unblemished wood floors, arching interior rafters, and full-length French windows giving onto a pool area and garden.

Mesmerized, she took three slow steps forward.

A *pool* on Tuckernuck, where the ecosystem was so fragile most residents barely flushed toilet paper into their plumbing systems. Who the hell did Todd Benson think he was?

Someone who paid other people to clean up his messes.

A wave of fury washed over her. Dionis glanced up, picking out the fiber optic camera blinking minutely from the crown molding, and raised both of her middle fingers to the most famous quarterback in America.

EIGHTEEN MINUTES LATER, Howie Seitz gave a shout of victory to his computer screen and punched his fist in the air.

"She's alive, goddamit! She's alive!"

"Officer," Todd Benson protested in his ear.

"That's your caretaker, Todd," Howie told him joyously, "and if you so much as *think* of filing a report of this break-in, the Nantucket Police will charge you with reckless endangerment and gross negligence. Send an insurance adjustor to your house, dude, and somebody to feed your horses. This girl is coming home."

He hung up without waiting for an answer. It was time to find the Potts brothers.

Chapter Twenty-Five

THE SUN SHONE on the morning of Peter Mason and
Meredith Folger's wedding, for the first time in four days.
A soft breeze tugged at branches that still rose sturdily
above the storm-pummeled gray outline of Nantucket
Island, and the sharp spire of the Congregational church
on Centre Street glinted in the light as though freshly
painted. The cobblestones and brick sidewalks dried out,
their colors bleached and faded from a scouring with
rainwater. Birds called to one another, reassured that the
gale had not entirely blown them to bits. People opened
doors and shook out rugs over back porches, lifting their
faces to the sun. They picked up the threads of plans that
had been interrupted unexpectedly, and ventured out on
bicycles to examine the sound and Atlantic beaches, the
turtles in Madaket's ponds.

At Bartlett's Farm, workers climbed ladders to
replace the panes of glass the wind had shattered in
acres of greenhouses. But the pumpkins were discovered
to be thriving in the fields, and the dahlia heads were
unbowed.

Sankaty Head Light and Great Point Light still stood,
as they seemed to have done forever. The floodwater was
receding, slowly, from the rocky base of Brant Point, and

a golden retriever named Tex was chasing a tennis ball in the shallows of Children's Beach.

Master Chief Boatswain's Mate Terry Samson finally had the day off, but a Watchstander alert on his cell phone at 8:38 A.M. informed him that a Hatteras Panacera named *Shytown* had been located off the south-western shore of Block Island. The local Coast Guard had impounded the vessel, which would be towed back to Nantucket pending police inquiries.

Dionis Mather slept late, in her own bed, and woke to find the pattern of sunlight on the ceiling of her room faintly puzzling. In sudden panic, she hurtled from beneath the coverlet and went to check on her father.

Jack was sitting in his usual chair in the kitchen with a mug of coffee and smiled when she appeared.

Howie Seitz, his short hair standing on end and his long fingers holding a piece of bacon, sat across from him. Howie smiled, too. Dionis remembered then that she had agreed to go with him to a wedding later. She kissed her father on the cheek and wondered what she would wear.

At 2:10 in the afternoon, Julia Mason arrived on the third flight out of LaGuardia to Nantucket that day, and demanded to be personally assisted down the plane steps to the tarmac. She wore an exotic pink fascinator on her perfectly coiffed head, worthy of the paparazzi at Windsor, and a Kelly bag over her arm.

Hale Whitney and his son Trey were waiting to meet her.

At his home in Siasconset, Sky Jackson loaded the last case of wines he'd chosen months earlier for the wedding reception into the back of his Porsche and checked his watch. His wife, Mayling, would be dressing the flower girls, Casey and Madeleine, on Cliff Road right about now, and making sure the bride's makeup did not stain the exquisite satin as it was lifted over her head. Woven of cream-colored silk with the faintest hint of chartreuse, it was perfect with Meredith's blonde hair, and swirled with a life of its own around her ankles.

Tess Starbuck loaded a second set of trays into her catering van and handed the keys to Brittany. She had trained the younger woman herself over the past two years, both at Greengage and in the kitchens of countless island clients; Brittany would get the feast started while Tess watched the exchange of vows.

Ralph Waldo Folger adjusted the set of his bow tie and reached to the upper shelf of his closet for a cherished straw boater. Together, he and John would walk Merry down the aisle.

Peter Mason had retired to his farmhouse after the previous night's rehearsal to observe an informal tradition—that the groom only see the bride for the first time on his wedding day as she walked down the aisle. He had slept soundly and taken a five-mile run through the moors well before breakfast. It was good to steal these few hours alone, without the raucous sideline comments of his nieces and nephews; to walk silently with his dog through the acres of bog and note that the brackish floodwaters were receding. Later, he shared a few fingers of Scotch with Rafe da Silva, their feet propped companionably on the rail of the back porch.

It was almost like old times.

Neither of them bothered to say much. Rafe was mentally composing his best man toast. Peter was considering the changeable shades of Meredith's green eyes, and wondering which hue her wedding dress would conjure. He hoped it paired well with the peridot and diamond earrings he had given her the previous night, after the rehearsal.

RALPH HAD BROUGHT his restored antique truck, a 1952 Chevy Bowtie painted a deep bottle green, with five bars of polished chrome for a grille, to drive Merry to the church in style. He had strewn the hood with a wreath of blue hydrangeas and ribbons that fluttered in the breeze. Her father was already waiting on Centre Street, to greet guests as they arrived. The Whitney boys, wearing Nantucket Reds and blue blazers from Murray's Toggery, were standing at the altar with their Uncle Peter. Casey and Madeleine wore pale blue and carried lightship baskets— woven by Ralph—filled with late summer flowers.

The florist's shipment had come through that morning, after all.

Merry held a few stems of perfect calla lilies, cream colored with chartreuse throats, as Mayling Stern had envisioned when she designed the wedding gown months ago. The stems were wrapped in chartreuse ribbon. Around her wrist Merry wore a gold bracelet of her grandmother Sylvie's, but at her ears were Peter's stones. Her blonde hair had been swept off her face and gathered in an elegant knot at the nape of her neck; another calla lily rested there.

Ralph Waldo pulled the truck to the curb of Centre Street and let down the tailgate to release the Whitney girls, who'd ridden the short distance from Cliff Road in the back. They shook out their skirts, lifted their baskets high, and allowed Ralph to swing them down from the flatbed. Then he opened Meredith's door and offered her, gallantly, his hand.

She stepped out, a princess in a pair of glass slippers.

In childhood, she'd always imagined her best friend Adelia Duarte lifting the train of a sumptuous gown and wrangling her veil into submission. But she had decided against a veil and Summer Hughes was her maid of honor, now. Merry spared a mental blessing for Del, who had died too young and released her memory on the island wind. Then she turned to Summer, who stood next to Ralph, and kissed her cheek.

The doctor looked glorious in a sea blue silk gown she'd chosen herself, her black hair waving over her shoulders. In a moment, the bridal party was positioned and waiting for the first chords of the organ.

Somewhere ahead, a soprano broke into "Ave Maria."

Casey looked over her shoulder and hissed at Madeleine. Holding their baskets as carefully as fresh ice cream cones, the two girls stepped forward.

John set his hand lightly under Meredith's right elbow, while Ralph cupped her left. They rose steadily up the broad, shallow steps of the Congregational church in time to the music, and passed from sunlight into shade.

LATER, AS THEY sat at a café in Montparnasse one perfect autumn evening, Peter asked if Merry had told her father and Ralph her news.

She shook her head, and took a sip of champagne. "Time enough to break it to them once we're back," she said.

"I figured you'd want to mull it over while you were gone. With enough distance to evaluate everything."

"It's a big decision."

"Yes," Peter said. "But one you've been moving toward for months, I think, if not years. What happened with Pocock makes it obvious."

Merry took his hand. "Are you okay with this? Really?"

"If it makes you happy—of course. I just want you to be sure. Before you throw your life into upheaval."

She drew a deep breath. "Change is terrifying, Peter. Which is why it's necessary. I'm so glad you're here, to help me through."

Peter lifted the bottle of champagne from its ice and refilled her glass. Then he lifted his in a toast.

"To you, Meredith. The next Chief Folger of the Nantucket Police."

Acknowledgments

TEN HURRICANES HAVE hit Massachusetts since 1851: five of them Category One, three Category Two, and two Category Three on the Saffir-Simpson Hurricane Wind Scale. The worst in recent memory was Hurricane Bob, which struck September 21, 1991, but the worst in generations was the Great New England Hurricane of 1938, which was a Category Five at its formation in the Atlantic and Cat Three when it made landfall. Tales of its devastation linger along the coast.

Unnamed, but seared in local memory, is what came to be called The Perfect Storm, after Sebastian Junger's nonfiction account of a combined nor'easter/cyclone that formed off Nova Scotia from the remnant of Hurricane Grace, in the days running up to Halloween, 1991. It did not make landfall, but is credited with waves that may have surged as high as one hundred feet, deadly to one particular swordfishing boat and crew caught on the Georges Bank.

Happily, no hurricane on record has made landfall directly on Nantucket, although the island is frequently ravaged by storms and their consequent damage. My account of Teddy in this novel is entirely fictitious, as is my creative interpretation of the hurricane's possible impact; my description of the preparations, official and private, that islanders might take in advance of such a natural disaster are, however, drawn from Nantucket's public preparedness websites and evacuation zone maps. I make no pretense to complete accuracy in portraying the impact of an island hurricane; the details are hypothetical, and I hope they remain so.

Life on Tuckernuck Island is one of Nantucket's cherished subjects of speculation. A few islanders who own boats sometimes graze the smaller island's shores, for fishing and hunting purposes, but few trespassers venture into the private world that remains discreetly guarded by its homeowners. The responses of Nantucketers, when I mentioned I was planning to visit Tuck, were predictable and almost comical—to a person, they stared at me openmouthed for a few seconds, before recovering enough to say, "I've always wanted to see that place. How are you getting over there?" Tuckernuck might as well have been the summit of Everest, or the dark side of the moon. It took me nearly a year of stumbling queries to arrange a visit myself.

I must therefore thank a group of people who agreed to share memories and a few facts about their cherished community. I am so grateful to Denver resident and friend Steve Coffin, a descendant of one of the four founding families of Nantucket and later Tuckernuck, who generously put me in touch with his network of Tuckernuck summer residents. These include Michael, who has been fortunate enough to spend part of every year of his life on Tuckernuck, along with generations of his family; Lorin, his childhood friend, who was often invited to the island for halcyon summers; and Margot, who has gathered her family for decades to vacation on Tuckernuck. (I omit their surnames for purposes of privacy.) I am deeply grateful to the Souza brothers, island caretakers who ferried me from Jackson Point to the Tuckernuck lagoon one bright July day, despite their obvious apprehension that I was a rank interloper committing some sort of scam. Their accounts of the details they have managed for years—from home repair and construction, to medical evacuation, garbage collection, lawn mowing, solar panel installation and the delivery of every last folding chair, flower arrangement, caterer and portable john required for a Tuckernuck wedding of over a hundred guests—were invaluable. Thanks also to Seth Levine of Nantucket for his willingness to help me penetrate Tuckernuck's veil. None of the people who talked to me is responsible in any way for my portrait of the island, or my errors in depicting it.

Anecdotes and assistance aside, I don't pretend to know what living on Tuckernuck is truly like, nor have I captured much in this story about the smaller island's extraordinary atmosphere. It is haunting in its isolation and beauty, the untamed cacophony of its flocks of birds, the stillness of its sudden woods, the wind stirring among its wetlands, unobserved by the world. I hope the people who treasure Tuckernuck are left happily to do so, in peace.

One night, a few summers ago on Nantucket, remains a warm memory: sitting around a candleflame at Dune, one of my favorite restaurants, during the Nantucket Book Festival. The people at that table—Mark, my husband; Rafe Sagalyn, my literary agent, and his wife, Anne; Juliet Grames, associate publisher of Soho Crime, and my editor on this novel; and Paul Oliver, head of

Soho's publicity department—have supported my work as a writer for years. I'm grateful to each of you. Thanks also to Soho publisher Bronwen Hruska, and to Rachel Kowal, who turned this manuscript into something that could be read.

Francine Mathews
September, 2019